D1120818

John Knowles' *A Separate Peace:*
BOOKMARKED

The *Bookmarked* Series

John Knowles' *A Separate Peace:*

BOOKMARKED

Kirby Gann

Kirby Gann, *Series Editor*

PUBLISHING

NEW YORK

Copyright © 2016 by Kirkby Gann Tittle.
All rights reserved.

No part of this book may be used or reproduced in any manner
without written permission of the publisher. Please direct inquires
to:

Ig Publishing
Box 2547
New York, NY 10163
www.igpub.com

ISBN: 978-1-63246-010-3 (paperback)

PRINTED IN THE UNITED STATES OF AMERICA
FIRST EDITION | FIRST PRINTING

You don't want a life based on your failure to understand life, right?
—Charles D'Ambrosio, "Salinger and Sobs"

WE DON'T GET TO CHOOSE WHERE WE COME FROM. Nor, for much of this life, do we get a say in determining the kind of person we are—I mean the bedrock foundational stuff—or are able to account for the differences between what we find pleasing and what we wish to avoid, what excites versus what fails to move us, whether we have courage or suffer congenital cowardice; nor do we get to select which experiences will prove formative and which will fade from memory. Time is helpful here. Only over time do we begin to suspect our available possibilities. With luck, in time we learn to recognize this delirious freedom that allows us to refine the best parts of ourselves, to move more in *this* direction instead of toward *that* one, to create the kind of person we wish to be. This is one of the cool things that come with being human and alive.

A writer's sensibility is honed not only via disciplined efforts at writing but also—maybe even more so—by what is read. Certain books work like strops whetting a blade, sharpening the fore-edge of our vision, widening the scope of what we might reach for in our own pages. Any writer can cop to that essential encounter when *this one book* changed

5

everything, when the story transformed from mere text to personal revelation, rolling away an intractable stone to reveal the path forward in our lives.

For me it was *A Separate Peace*. I freely acknowledge it's not the sexiest title to choose for this brief exploration into origins. Yet it is the most honest one, and in this instance I don't think the decision is mine to make; it feels as though the book chose me. It was here before I was, anyway.

It even seems unlikely to me now that a brief, quiet novel about the friendship between two boys at a New England prep school during the Second World War's crucial year of 1942 has held sway over my sensibilities as a novelist for nearly three decades. Especially unlikely as *A Separate Peace* wasn't a book I returned to again and again over those years, retrieved to study how its various elements worked, or to imitate its voice or structures, pry it apart the way writers do to better understand how to put together a work of fiction. Reading for example and instruction has been my habit and process with nearly every book read since my teen years: on one level looking for the usual pleasures and transport, on another searching for clues to how to better my own efforts at putting words on paper; even, admittedly—and if the book is any good—hard on the lookout for what I might steal outright. (Every writer does this whether or not they are willing to concede it.) Nor have I ever returned to those pages for the simple pleasure of reacquainting myself with a story remembered as one deeply enjoyed in my youth.

It's a peculiar thing about books: we don't get to decide which ones affect us most. We don't choose which stories stay with us after the cover is closed and the book is returned to the shelf, or loaned out to one of those friends who never return what they borrow. No one gets to determine what experiences prove fundamental to who they are.

Some books don't overwhelm or especially impress us at the moment of reading them, and yet as time passes we come to realize that they have never entirely gone away—they haven't slipped into that twilight realm of titles we're pretty sure we've read but maybe need to hear the gist of again to be sure. Quiet books of this nature don't prove their ultimate value until later, often for years after we believe we have moved on. It's as though such books don't reveal their singular power until we've managed to live enough life and collect enough reading experience to be able to situate them properly, to see what shape they've made for themselves in our interior lives.

It can be difficult to express why. No doubt a lot of this has to do with who we are when we encounter the book in question. Anyone who reads can identify that special frisson that accompanies the rare synchronization of art and life when you sink into not only a good book but the perfect one, it's the *right* book at the *right* time, the book in your hands feels written specifically for you to read at this moment in your life and it addresses only matters that interest you, and in language that delights and yet feels like it could have sprung from your own head—if only you'd had the chance to give voice to it; if only you'd had the proper idea to get you started. The perfect book persuades you of truths only suspected before. The difference between a book and the *right* book feels analogous to the difference between casual lovers and the moment of falling in love. *Amazement* might be the most useful descriptive word. A sensation all the more amazing for having been inspired by something as simple as a story.

•

"We tell ourselves stories in order to live" is one of many lines for which Joan Didion has been justly celebrated. Not only because it's pithy and to the point and easy to remember. Yet it's a remark I've never felt entirely comfortable with; I veer back and forth between resistance and embrace, between mocking its crusty stench of empty platitude and accepting her words with my typical, characteristic ambivalence. The line comes up a lot in literary circles, reliably delivered by someone in workshops and lectures and conferences. Often enough that one might feel obligated to have some rejoinder ready at hand. I'm unsure of the remark's context, if she said it in an interview or inscribed it in one of her extraordinary essays; on the one hand it's irksome, a brash overstatement claiming greater cultural territory and importance for the all-cap WRITER, insinuating that it is only through literature that we are humanized, and only through story can we make sense of the world we live in, etc.—a claim that many days I struggle to accept. It's apropos applied to my own life, certainly—I cannot imagine who I would be without my having read Dostoevsky, Bolaño, Nabokov, Kafka et al, and my life has not only been enriched by such classics but also by innumerable novels of mystery and suspense, the noir and detective genres—yet I see proof in the lives of friends and family that it *is* possible to lead a deep, rewarding, meaningful life without having read any of the great novelists. Without having read any novels at all.

Then I wonder if what Didion meant was the use of stories as tools, literally, for creating our selves. A widespread view among psychologists and some philosophers involves the concept of "narrative identity," a theory that we bring a sense of unity to our lives by creating narratives for them, providing coherence and purpose to our ever-evolving experience of everyday living. Each individual narrative constructs a past, a history in which we are the hero, the inviolable center, and, by posing causal links, the mind connects that past to the present as we perceive it and as circumstances demand. Via this stance we can imagine a future toward which we try to direct ourselves. In that sense, yeah, sure, to live is to tell ourselves stories; stories bring order to the chaotic mess of who we are.

The implications of such internalized self-storytelling can get weird, though. "Narrative Identity"—the notion that the self is a story—implies we must have a clear beginning (okay, creative writers: aside from being born, what would be your "initiating event"?); a middle, where things get complicated and we enter into what the ancient Greeks called the *agon*, pitching ourselves into struggles we either overcome, fail to meet, or respect as a draw; this, it follows, leads to an end, a denouement, one that evolves naturally (if we are to be a story well-told) from all that has come before. Which I guess would be death. Nothing seems more natural than dying.

Yet whose life holds such coherence? In the sense that one thing naturally gives rise to the next? I am in my late forties as I write this, and have plenty of personal history from which to derive a narrative and construct a self. But it's hardly an overstatement to say there isn't much in the way of unity; memories float to the fore of my random-access mind and sink down again, discreet episodes bouncing around the years, linked sometimes by an image / subject rhyme scheme more often—if linked at all—than establishing any kind of narrative coherence. The center holding my story together is the bald fact of my physical body, that all my experiences have occurred to this nervous system, this set of heart, lungs, and ever-wandering mind, but the circumstances offer little narrative direction aside from time and aging. I can look to any number of moments and label them formative to my identity. For example, the memory of my mid-twenties self being startled, at first even frightened, on a midnight beach stroll by the sudden movement of a man-sized shadow standing calf-deep in the waves as I happened near. I stopped without meaning to, as though the sight of that still form several yards away required I mirror it, the both of us stuck on sudden alert. Then my instinct for self-defense suddenly transformed to fascination, even awe, as the silhouette fell forward yet without crashing into the water and for an instant seemed suspended in space, an action my mind couldn't make any immediate sense of. It looked like the figure was throwing off a blanket of some kind that caught in the wind—exact detail was impossible in that dark and with that distance—and then the instant found its coherence, the blanket changed to wings, the strange man-figure became a bird taking flight low above the breakers, the beat of those wings heavier and louder than the waves rolling over my feet.

My first great blue heron, and a great (because unexpected) moment of intimate witness to the majesty of the wild. A city boy, I'd never encountered an animal of that size outside of a zoo, and never at such proximity, the heron passing close enough to push a breeze across my cheek, filling my nostrils with a gamey marine scent.

This, set against a recent moment in which again I was made unexpected witness, this time sweating heavily, heaving breath on an obscure trail through park woods near my home, where I run most summer evenings. I'd stopped, struck still by an irregular jabbing movement at the edge of my vision and the sound of sudden disturbance in the quiet water of Beargrass Creek, a rivulet that feeds the Ohio and cuts a deep and winding swathe through my city. At the edge of one steep bank I caught the flight of another great blue heron seeking to escape my presence, and again it was the heavy heft of large wings over water, a resonant hush, three or four wingbeats and then a stately gliding upward to reach an overhanging alder branch upstream. I walked slowly toward the tree to get a better look, and the sunlight angling through the trees glinted on the silver scales of a fish dangling from either side of the bird's lance-like beak before being tossed up and sucked down the long question mark of the heron's throat. The bird's yellow eyes blinked in contentment a few times before then coming to cautiously regard me.

Such a strange, prehistoric-looking bird, with it's stalk legs and shaggy feathers sprouting disarranged like so much unkempt, tousled hair. The stillness of the heron astounds me; once so composed, the bird appeared to become an aspect of the alder itself, and easy to overlook if my eyes hadn't followed it on the path it took to get there. For what seemed like several moments the city surrounding us fell away and we were two singular living beings, one wild, one not, each silently taking in the other, until I stepped slowly to the base of the tree to see how close it would allow me to come. Evidently the heron did not share the same fascination for me that I felt for it, though, and with its peculiar grace it leaned forward into the air and sailed back down the creek until I could only make it out via its movement among the summer green, and then lost sight of it altogether in all the leaves atop leaves. In that view my head made an easy transition into picturing the world without me—without any of us—and what the planet must have been like eons ago with trees and streams full of such sights, what extraordinary brutal and violent beauty the planet must have teemed with then.

I take these two instances of direct encounters with herons, both of which were intense and invigorating experiences (for me) marked by that kind of awe that comes with any close-up interaction with the indifferent wild, especially the "great" or unusual wild—the one beyond squirrels and robins and cardinals puttering about their business in my yard—and pronounce them *formative* in that both instances occurred at a time of great doubt and loneliness; they construct a slant rhyme scheme to my life, and tempt me to pursue some level of meaning in that both times I came upon this bird known for its solitude when evaluating the marked degree of my own isolation. What meaning might there be? The natural world mirrors my inner one, as though making commentary? It wishes to remind me that in solitude one can still thrive, be a thing of beauty?

I recognize such grasping at meaning is entirely a construction of my own mind struggling to assert its centrality to the universe, that solitary bird / lonesome man are no more than random coincidences, the likelihood of which could be formulated probably into an equation by another mind more gifted than my own. Neither memory connects to who I am and have become.

The supposed memories that would build my narrative identity should be memories of a different kind, I suppose—

memories of similarly intense events that have modeled me into this man sitting with a keyboard on his lap at this precise moment. And yet a case could be made that those salient events, and the identification of them as salutary to my becoming, are similarly selected, their meaning foisted upon them by my choosing. Couldn't a case be made that my two close run-ins with (what seems to me) an exotic bird are in fact formative experiences? One can construct a narrative however one wants and derive from it some attendant meanings, but these meanings leave me ambivalent to their objective veracity; yes, I can argue, my sense of my past allows for a sense of unity to my current self, yet I'm not entirely convinced that I'm getting to an impartial truth of what brought me to this self.

In particular this leads me to a similar ambivalence about the experiences that unify my sense of a writing self—a self I value, encourage, and protect fiercely even during the long stretches when not much writing is getting done. It has become and has long been the self that provides me most with purpose, the one that gives the deepest sensation of personal evolution, this sense of *moving toward something important,* and but also it confounds me because I don't know exactly why this should be the case. "The writing self"—and by this I don't mean diary / journal / letter-writing, but the conscious undertaking of creating narratives that hopefully others, even strangers, might read and find stimulating, moving, artful—is an often unpleasant one wracked by doubts, anxieties, frustrations and failures, an identity often saddled with the suspicion that none of what it does actually needs to be done anymore, and certainly not by me; an identity consistently tempted to extinguish itself; a temptation held off by the final question: If not this (the writing), then what? The lack of a clear answer often leads to more writing.

This kind of circular ruminating (the above paragraph cannot be termed *reasoning*) prompts me to wonder what experiences proved formative to the creation of this writer. I do believe a writer is formed and not born; we may be born with a natural strength for language, say, for the sounds of certain words arranged melodically, but that's a far cry from all that's required for the creation of worthwhile novels, stories, narratives of any kind, such as this one is struggling to become, or even for the harboring of a desire to wrestle with the making of these things. In personal terms, inspecting early experiences suggests I could have turned out quite differently. I can construct a narrative identity that lends coherence to my being a writer, true, but could also construct one in which I turned out otherwise. I could have turned out as another kind of man were it not for the formative experience of certain books at certain times. *A Separate Peace* by John Knowles was the first of these.

·

Aside from my personal history cohering around this same body as it has changed in time, this same brain as it has struggled to grow and remember and accept and decide, my "narrative identity" seems to hold many lives, separate unities, disparate desires. The identity of the son, the brother, the friend, and lover, and husband; the innocent child and infuriating adolescent and uncertain young man; the musician, the athlete, the reader; the heartbroken and the briefly fulfilled. Mix these many selves with the consistently self-conscious daydreamer self and perhaps only one identity could bring fragile unity to them all: the writer. *The writer* is what constructs a cogent narrative from all the other strands. Yet isn't it peculiar then that this self is the one I've struggled most to accept; it's like I fell into writing through the narrowing options of other avenues. I could have "evolved" into so many different selves than the one, evidently, I seem to have turned out to have become.

Everyone has a moment in history which belongs particularly to him.

—A Separate Peace

MORE THAN LIFE EXPERIENCE, MORE THAN INHERENT imagination, books come from other books. *A Separate Peace* arrived at a time when the power of books was only beginning to take hold of me, their quiet influence literally sustaining my mind and imagination for years, long before the notion of trying to write one—to write anything beyond teenage rock lyrics / "poems"—reared its intimidating head. I cannot pinpoint precisely what age this happened to be—adolescence, at least; fourteen, fifteen, whatever the conventional high school age is for a freshman or sophomore in English class. At the time I was no more certain about my future as a writer, or what was required "to become" a writer, or even if I honestly *enjoyed the act of writing,* than I was certain about anything else at that age. Who is? 1982, 1983: there were many selves at work bouncing for attention, many other possible futures available when the county system bussed me downtown to start at Central High School, a morose yellow-brick structure that from outside looked more like a warehouse or factory than a place of learning, located in the center of downtown among the low-income housing of the Village West apartments.

There, for a dollar, you could buy joints made mostly of tobacco with some weed mixed in from the older boys who hung out beside pristine Cadillacs and BMWs in sleeveless undershirts across the street from the school parking lot. Making your way inside, half-asleep and bent under the weight of your book bag, you passed through clouds of acrid cigarette smoke and the heavier scent of pot, head down to insure you didn't make eye contact with any of those upperclassmen who liked to snag freshman belongings and scatter textbooks across the pavement for a laugh.

Central was not a place that suggested auspicious futures or encouraged long hours of studious contemplation, the honing of young minds. It was a place to avoid eye contact, stick to your own side of the hallway, and move quickly to reach the relative sanctuary of the classroom.

I loved it. The charge of the atmosphere, the threat of violence either suffered or witnessed, the thrilling noise from multiple hand-held radios vying for prominence between classes, the shoulder-to-shoulder interaction with different races—whites were a minority there, and the school's ESL program was flush in refugees from southeast Asia and the middle east—excited and intimidated me after a childhood in which the one or two black students in a class had made for a mild curiosity at first, and then became an unremarkable difference. Central, however, was the kind of place where a smart kid kept on the move, no time for stopping and staring for a second without being confronted by someone inevitably larger bellowing, *What you looking at?*

You can get used to anything once the newness wears off. You learn your place in the hierarchy of things. So long as you stayed there, you were fine. The volatile atmosphere in the hallways, cafeteria, and parking lot was one in which even a quasi-suburban white kid active in his Episcopal church and raised on poolside summers could come to thrive, once he learned where he belonged.

•

I was an impatient and hyperactive kid who ran everywhere anyway, even between rooms at home, lacking the discipline to sit quiet for long. The patience and stillness required to write has never come naturally; it's an acquired, self-trained behavior, an essential that in all honesty still fails me from time to time, my body unable to settle, the prospect of sitting down in a chair at my desk for what will be hours unappetizing. There are biographies of triumphant artists where the subject seems born to literature, ambitious with the pen and blooming verse and story even before puberty, indulged and encouraged by a doting mother, usually, and intellectually rapacious at the outset. This would not be me. To be the boy who scribbled away at stories and novels in personal notebooks, or wrote out plays to be performed for the family and neighbors, would have required hours of stillness and willful contemplation that my childhood self did not possess the capacity to undergo. I was impulsive, thoughtless, and often corrected, the kind of child forever being lectured on the necessity of considering the consequences of his actions, to try to think for once before acting.

Hints and intimations can be found, though, in retrospect. But hints found only with the knowledge of a life immersed in literature as an adult, only an eye in search of such roots would identify them as such; otherwise—should my adult self had found his way into another avocation—these same incidents and tendencies would be mere random facts of a childhood. My mother, a former elementary school teacher who for much of her life came dangerously close to being a hoarder, kept samples of school assignments she found especially charming— or *precious,* to use her word of choice—from the early years of both her sons. These are rather humiliating to go over now, but something's there, a preoccupation, let's say, that implies a particular mind's becoming. It seems I had a peculiar empathy for inanimate objects. When directed to write a story I must have felt the need to give voice to the voiceless, to the inner lives of appliances such as the washing machine and dryer, and the outdoor furniture, or even the rocks in the drainage ditch that ran between our back yard and the back yards of houses on the other side of the block. A thread runs through these pieces in their self-consciousness and the boisterous expression of anxieties, fears that the speakers couldn't live up to what all was expected of them, their tasks thankless, exhausting, lonely, and often pointless. Having no memory of writing any of these exercises, what I glean from them is the mind of an unexceptional child stressing already over the threat of failing to meet expectations, coupled with an existential bent. None of these "stories" run more than twenty lines or so, and read as though dashed off—likely written under the demand to finish before being allowed to go outside and play.

Maybe it's being too generous as well to call these assignments *stories;* the writing teacher in me now would call them character sketches, or brief monologues. What's of some interest to me here is the recognition that this form is precisely how I begin work as an adult on any new draft: starting with a voice, a vaguely discerned character, and listening to what she or he has to say, my instincts out to discover their predicament. And these early exercises also display the same weakness that continues to cause me problems when drafting something new in that not a lot happens, it's a recounting of what preoccupies the speaker without a word of what brought him to this moment or what he plans to do; there's no arc to the drama, no concrete acts; mostly we read of a consciousness asserting its plight. Wishing to be understood. A washing machine asking the reader to understand the intrinsic difficulties of meeting the expectations demanded of washing machines everywhere. The struggle to get something to happen on the page, evidently, has been my burden from the beginning; often I overcompensate for this shortcoming by making too much happen too quickly, without proper establishment of motivation or clear cause, whenever I'm not droning on about what some character is like, or what she thinks, until it feels like a reader could find more dynamic action in a Beckett novel.

Another early signal: in first grade the school held a poetry contest, with the winning poem to be submitted to compete against every other public elementary school throughout the county. I forget what they gave as a prize, or if they gave anything other than the recognition of having been deemed the best. (I speak of a time before kids received awards for participation; this was the early seventies, when public education wasn't geared toward encouraging self-esteem. Rather the presumption was that second place or even outright failure were realities everyone needed to come to terms with early on, and if your self-esteem suffered accordingly then you were expected to try harder next time, or else come to accept your place in the implicit hierarchy of the class, the school, the world.)

The teacher passed out the wide-ruled paper that I disliked because of its grayish natural fiber and waxy finish— even then I liked bright white, high-contrast paper—against which the standard No. 2 pencil hardly stood out, and it felt awkwardly slick, too, so that your pencil slipped all over the surface. You had to press down hard to make a clear mark and the paper ripped easily and often. Maybe it had been designed for use with crayons; we used the same paper for the art projects that eventually ended up on the refrigerator door at home. Already I'd developed preferences for different paper bonds and finishes.

I don't remember what we were told about writing poems or how much time the teacher set aside for us to come up with our verses. It seemed like a long time, and I wasn't interested; I thought poetry had to be about flowers and trees and nature, and vaguely understood it had to be geared toward girls (or a girl), and love—all things I considered with great ambivalence. Every head in the classroom bent to the task while mine remained up, astonished by how everyone seemed to know immediately, judging by the rapid movement of their hands, what they wanted to say. There was a boy in the class whose name I've forgotten, but likely you know him, too—every K–12 classroom in my experience presented some version of him: the strange one with a body that looked put together with mismatched parts, skinny with outsized feet and pants that always revealed the snug white tube socks above his clunky black shoes, an obscurely unclean vibe about his being, his unwashed hair and bits of food in his teeth. When he spoke, saliva gathered and dried in the edges of his mouth. Let's call him Steve. I noticed Steve had inclined his head toward his desk but, unlike the others, he was only pretending to work, his left hand making motions over the paper without the pencil touching it, the waxy finish reflecting the overhead lights. With his other hand he went about the real action: picking at a scab on his ear.

Steve had a serious compulsion about that ear. Twice already that year he had picked and pinched until it bled, once in copious enough amounts that stopping the bleeding became the classroom's main concern until the teacher could get him out of there. He had two wounds high on the helix and parallel to one another like fangs had gotten to him, and I could see today he was committed to catching a break from this assignment via bleeding out again.

A poster banner ran three-quarters of the circumference of the room, just below the ceiling, illustrating the world's geologic eras from the Precambrian to the Holocene. Like many kids, even back in the 1970s before Hollywood created such vivid and lifelike versions of them, I was fascinated by dinosaurs, to the extent that I'd missed the phase of wanting to be a fireman or police officer when I grew up, and told any adults who inquired that maybe I'd be a "dinosaur man." I remember asking if there were in fact jobs of this nature out in the world, which is how I learned the meaning and pronunciation of the words *archaeology* and *paleontology* probably earlier than most. A lengthy portion of the poster depicted the Mesozoic era and grew interestingly more detailed—at least to my eyes—at its Triassic and Jurassic periods, the best times, when most of the great dinosaurs roamed.

The teacher announced that we were closing in on the deadline to turn in our poems. She reminded us to write our names and classroom number in the upper right-hand corner of the paper. That classic fear, that surge of panic that came with being called to deliver at a moment of complete and woeful unpreparedness—an alarm with which I would come to grow deeply accustomed over the following years, to the point that it seemed a necessary stage to getting any assignment done—rinsed through me.

I hadn't written a word yet and already we were near the finish. So I went with what what my mind held, blood and dinosaurs, and tackled the demands of rhyme through a kind of sprung rhythm:

> Dinosaurs, Dinosaurs,
> they're what I know. Some
> really did grow.
> What did they do? They ate you.
>   Help!

I make no claims that my first literary effort revealed some inchoate genius, or even talent. We all have to start somewhere. But the poem did go on to be selected as the representative poem from Hikes Elementary, grades 1–5, and then somehow won the county-wide contest as well. To the ecstatic thrill of my parents, one of the local papers printed it in the Metro/Neighborhoods section above my misspelled name, along with finalists. The first publication, and thus the initial step of this illustrious career. Here we could claim the young writer was on his way, the pathway forward set—my parents surely would—but in reality this small accomplishment was only something else that happened to a boy easily distracted, unfocused, and interested in so many other things. That the award had been unexpected, even unsought, gave it a unique charm. It brought a good deal of attention and praise from adults, and there was a satisfaction in seeing the newspaper column wafting beneath the Snorkeldorf magnet every time I opened and shut the refrigerator door. As a future "dinosaur man" in embryo, however, I had fossils to search out in the wide drainage ditch behind the house. Perhaps the strange creatures of the Freakies cereal line (Snorkeldorf, Hamhose, Grumble and Cowmumble, among others) had correlations in the prehistoric record yet to be discovered. Such explorations took precedence over scribbled verse.

·

I believe writers are more often made than born; still, natural predilections must exist as well, aspects of character that contingency happens to nurture as we begin to take possession of ourselves. A factor common among author biographies is a significant amount of time early in life spent alone, often in convalescence. Which probably accounts for why most people who *don't* read picture the typical writer as some friendless pasty-necked geek. My own history contains both, although the stretch of convalescence did not occur until my early twenties when a severe back injury returned me to a floor in my parents home for several weeks, where gifted books piled up beside me. Writing had already captured my interest by then and so the physical suffering was offset by the opportunity to read for hours without interruption. But going farther back—diving deeper into my own navel is how this feels—I find many of my most lasting memories from childhood are steeped in imaginary lives. Every kid plays like this, inventing imaginary friends or reciting storylines for dolls or action figures to enact, and there's probably some name for this stage of development that my childlessness excuses me for never having had to learn. Anyway, as we age and mature and reality begins to impose its incessant demands we indulge less often in such harmless myth-making, learn to put away childish things, etc.

A fiction writer, though, never gets around to moving on. Rather than it being a stage of development, this habit of play settles in as an important facet of who one is. How else to describe the invention of stories populated by imaginary people but as a kind of semi-directed daydreaming? The lure of this kind of play remains provocative to those of the writerly bent, even compulsive and habitual; the process clings to the same rites as childhood but the focus changes, turns less whimsical and by necessity more coherent, oriented toward adult possibilities and concerns. In some way—and this is neither for good or ill, it simply *is*, as the nature of the process—one's character remains deformed from that supposed maturity, reluctant (or unable) to move beyond the detailed imagining of other, vastly foreign selves. We can't experience firsthand everything available, every interesting possibility, in this world. So through sympathetic imagination we invent other selves.

As Oscar Wilde wrote: "One's real life is so often the life one does not lead." Fiction writers try their hands at several different lives and try to get to the truth at the bottom of each of them—lives that often become more "real" than their very own, at least for hours at a time.

What I'm thinking about is different from the convention of, say, pretending to be a star athlete while playing basketball with friends, when everyone takes turns mimicking the sports announcer with the game clock ticking down. In my own case I would call out, "Griffith picks up the ball and takes it to the hole" (Darrell Griffith being the name every twelve-year-old Kentucky boy had on his tongue the spring and summer of 1980, as he had led the University of Louisville to its first NCAA championship that year) and then move into the slow-motion of highlight films for a down-to-the-wire winning basket. "Doctor Dunkenstein again!" Someone else would be Dr. J, Magic Johnson, or Larry Bird, and for those instants in the game that's who we were, bearing the glory of exploits seen on TV while knowing no more about the players' lives than we knew of what our parents lives were like once they left for work. We might switch identities at a whim, just as a new name sprang to mind. Once the games finished, we returned to our regularly-scheduled identities, smiling at the thought of what it must feel like to be so unambiguously great at something as to inspire awe in everyone watching. None of this connects to what Wilde wrote; in fact this was its opposite, the impossible fantasy of those momentary lives being a large part of their allure.

On my own and left to my own devices, however, imagined selves could be so deeply inhabited as to replace the boy imagining them, accruing the details not only of storylines but personal histories: on the overgrown banks of that backyard ditch and stripped to a pair of shorts and no shoes, I might be an Indian brave cut off from his tribe by the movements of

Custer's army, trying to read daylight stars to find my way to safety while also making reconnaissance of the enemy's location; a pirate from England, the only survivor of a shipwreck caused by a necessary mutiny which grew out of hand, living flotsam who kissed the earth once he washed ashore, only to be taken prisoner by local authorities who then made him a slave (I named my pirate Edward Bonney and even construed an ersatz pirate costume from ripped trousers and an old wine-stained tuxedo shirt of my father's several sizes too big, a bright red bandanna wrapped around my head). Before the movies introduced us to Indiana Jones, I was archaeologist Clifton Banks, scouring the ditch for fossils while keeping hid from the primitive tribes who protected their ancestral land. This guise sank so deeply into me that it influenced my actual dreams. In one that recurred for years I stumbled into an extraordinary discovery there in the drainage ditch behind our house. Beneath the riprap stone of culvert ballast that we neighborhood kids deployed for the construction of small dams, I uncovered a hidden cave entrance. I slithered along a narrow passage—too narrow for an adult— to where the cave opened into a great hall, and on the walls there the skeletons of several dinosaurs, many never seen or recorded before, stood out perfectly preserved as if in amber, mutedly aglow as though beneath recessed museum lighting, so long undisturbed that even the pores of flesh could be made out embedded in the stone. The long hallway narrowed and seemed to close and then open again the deeper I wandered, an endless honeycomb of rooms reaching farther back in time with each successive cavern, the animal history of the earth portrayed in its walls as clearly as that poster remembered strung beneath the ceiling on three walls of my first-grade classroom.

A world underground and the possibilities to be discovered there proved a longstanding fascination. Maybe because the area in which we lived appeared so orderly, planned, every house with its eighth-of-an-acre lawn drawn with clipped boxwoods or taxus hedges and punctuated by a single oak or maple or holly, each house itself a slight variation on the ranch split-level template. Years would pass before I came to suspect that the real curiosities occurred in the lives of the families who resided behind the doors and bay windows of all that bricked and shuttered sameness. At my young age, though, what lurked out of sight and worthy of exploration lay under everyone's feet. That's where all the adventure awaited. Many times I dipped into the cabinet where we kept useful necessities for the eventual power outage—the usual thunderstorms or even strong winds could be counted on to return the neighborhood to nineteenth-century living several times every spring and summer—and grabbed the flashlight along with replacement batteries (because you never knew how long batteries would last), taking care to shut the drawer carefully so that it didn't appear disturbed in case my mother swept by. I didn't want to field questions of what I was doing with a flashlight in the middle of a summer day.

Then I would venture out alone into one of the many culverts embedded around the neighborhood, these concrete tunnels which in my imagination transformed into the interior of a lost ziggurat, a labyrinth to be searched for the treasures of a people mysteriously disappeared. Surely someone must have lived around here before the area was developed—didn't people live everywhere, all the time? So went my thinking. It was a small step then to enter those dark passages that connected one to another, slink past the scribbled and sprayed graffiti beyond where the light gave out, and slip into a maze of cold concrete, the useful bandanna now wrapped over my mouth as protection against the moldy air. For hours I crawled, or else walked hunched over into the darkness, guessing at my location by the faint light falling through the intermittent curbside grates, junctions walled by what seemed to be ancient red brick. No real reason *why* behind this desire, aside from curiosity and a vague awareness that such adventures would be forbidden by my parents, and might not even be exactly legal; but I wanted to see.

You learn what fears you have to confront when on your own in the dark. Throw a stone and it disappears, clacking away without much of an echo. That distant rumble closing in could be a flash flood raging forth or a truck roaring by overhead. Switch off the flashlight and remain absolutely still, squat down on throbbing knees and listen to a silence more absolute than ever imagined, take in the darkness so complete you cannot see your hand in front of your face, not even after long minutes of waiting for your eyes to adjust; only the memory of what was seen before extinguishing the light gives any idea of where you are and what's around you. Even though you hadn't been taking particular note of where you've been or where you were headed, your mind presents a map like an opaque blueprint and you find that just so very interesting, and wonder if everyone's brain works the same or only yours. Consider what you would do next if you dropped the flashlight now, or found that it won't turn back on. See how long you can go without freaking out before testing the switch. Try not to think about the possible difficulties of finding your way out.

Always the important moment came in which I recognized having reached a certain point where retracing my steps without getting lost still presented a plausible option; there were junctions everywhere down there, different tunnels, different directions to select. After a few such decisions it seemed unlikely I could make my way back without getting lost. I would pause a moment and replay where I'd made a right turn, where a left, always with the comforting picture in mind of how the distant light would look at the culvert's mouth— faintly perceptible and infinitely small at first, then growing into a riotous beacon as I imagined scrabbling my way nearer. I say "imagined" because it had to be, I never saw this actually happen. Never once did I turn around to go back the way I came. For whatever reason the flashlight beam kept pulling me forward, a separate tunnel would present itself, and then another one and then another, and I moved forward with the faith that an exit would be on offer when an exit was needed, a pliable manhole cover or loose grate waiting at the ready for when I made my way out.

Clifton Banks never made any discoveries of lasting note among the detritus scattered around down there. In those long pauses with the light turned off he would think of his children at home, of his wife who had argued with him not to go this time, that she had a bad feeling about him going to this unknown and ancient place. He would think of his family and wonder what they were doing at that exact same moment in which he hardly existed, breathing bad air through his trusty bandanna. He thought of his colleagues at the university and the uncertainty of his position there, not confidant he had their due respect despite that the department's very existence owed much to the value of his earlier discoveries. He sat in that absolute dark and wondered what the likelihood was, should he die right now, that anybody would ever find him, or know what had happened to him—and he didn't mind the prospect of this, it seemed fitting in a way, though he knew it would crush his youngest daughter Bettina, who believed he ruled the world.

My faith in finding a way out was always rewarded. There the story would end, as I regained my place in full sunlight and open air on some unfamiliar street, sometimes with an audience of other kids struck still by this person crawling out from underground, no longer the intrepid explorer but just another twelve-year-old in need of a shower once he figured his way back home.

·

There were other selves with lives as detailed as Bonney and Banks and Indian braves—a soldier in World War II (always in that war, never the more recent Vietnam, which seems odd to me now; maybe because of the landscape difference?), a traveling pianist with a taste for the blues; my mother claimed that I used to regale her with stories of my life as a teenaged girl who had been killed in a car wreck, telling her about the boys I'd liked at school and my father's job at a supermarket and totally weirding her out, though I have no memory of this at all.

The purpose of these selves and their stories—if "purpose" is a legitimate term to ascribe to them, and not merely me dispatching a meaning to them out of some need—probably has to do with figuring out the story of who I was. Which I submit as a primary cause in creating fiction at all: by throwing ourselves into other lives, we can get to the truth of who we are.

The question then becomes how to account for where these other selves came from; it wasn't like my own life was not interesting, or lacked absorbing things to do. There was no boring or stressful reality to escape from, nor any reason for my paleontological interests and sewer explorations not to be carried out by the boy I was. Perhaps it's that even at that early age the parameters of a single life felt too confining; I longed to be elsewhere and else-wise. For this I credit—or blame, depending on how one looks at it—books. We weren't a family of heavy TV watchers except during the college basketball and pro football seasons, and my narrative tendencies must have come from somewhere, influencing me toward becoming a boyish Emma Bovary or a Don Quixote with a ten-year-old's interests.

I thought any story or self by its nature required being far different from the story or self I was living. It wasn't until the novel *A Separate Peace* that the possibility of a worthwhile story could be made from sources and details near to my own experience occurred to me—belatedly. So much of the intensity of an encounter with a book is wrapped up in the time we meet it, the moment of who we are and what's going on in our own lives. It would be years before the John Knowles novel would make its way into my hands, but once it did, the impression was as though my entire reading life had been a readying to meet this specific story.

•

Books were a constant in our house, a presence in nearly every room, and never intended as mere decoration or furnishing but as active objects for everyone to engage with. Still no one would have described the family as a literary one. Despite the minor accomplishments asserted in the sections above, no one would argue that I'd been groomed to write. The parents would come to encourage and support the idea of having a writer in the family only later, once I'd finished college—a time when they probably felt need to praise ambition of any kind in their youngest, having grown alarmed by his lack of interest exhibited toward the pursuit of some career deemed appropriate for any person "armed with a degree," as they described it. How to make a living was an often-expressed concern as well. Our family presented no precursors to the vocation for comparison; there were no eccentric ink-stained uncles or aunts, no grandfather who spouted drunken verse at holiday gatherings, and we didn't spend our evenings arrayed around the living room as father read us stories from the Bible or Twain or whatever. I never saw either of my parents write anything beyond a check, a letter (usually outraged) to a teacher, or a hurried note to tuck inside a thank-you card like any good upstanding Episcopalian would be expected to do.

What they did was practice a combination of enthusiastic support and "let them find their own way" over my brother and me throughout our childhoods, provoking us to discover our own interests by providing the opportunities to do so. In particular these opportunities broke down along the lines of arts, particularly music, and athletics: we were competitive swimmers before either of us had reached the age of ten, and although I never grew accustomed to that first cold bone-brittling smack of pool water that started each six AM practice, we became adept at the sport; my brother briefly held the city record for the fifty-meter backstroke. In middle school he took up cross-country running whereas I, reaching middle school two years behind him, took up soccer, being too small to make a go at football or basketball.

Our parents were of the type that attended every match or competition in which we engaged. They were vocal in the stands or along the pool, tribally loyal not only to their sons but to the teams they were a part of—mother prided herself on having been a cheerleader (captain of the squad) herself in college, and believed in team spirit. She inspired, embarrassed, and probably even offended other parents who weren't as gung-ho in their support of their own kids. Often she received an award of her own at the end-of-season banquets for her fervor and commitment, these awards she would laugh off as she made a point of congratulating us for the haul of trophies that seemed to come our way at the end of every season. Competitive sports took on a great coordinating force in our house and our parents were happy to encourage it, not only for the structure and socialization it gave, but likely for its physically draining effects as well, which led to less violent competition between their two sons at home once the hormones kicked in.

But they did not want to raise empty-headed jocks, either: schoolwork, studies, and at least *some* exposure to the arts was mandatory. We took to it naturally, I guess, the way most children do if introduced properly, without demand or pressure. It was my brother Jamie who set the standard. In fact, looking back to this early time, one could have been forgiven for predicting he would be the more likely to follow the line my own life has taken, as Jamie was the more naturally inclined to pass the hours with books, a lean figure kicked back quietly in his room with his feet up on the desk reading Frank Herbert's

Dune or anything by Tolkien, Bradbury, or Heinlein. Harry Harrison's *The Stainless Steel Rat* series was a particular favorite that he tried to turn me on to, but I could never get past the hokey factor of so much that's in science fiction—whenever starships and distant, invented planets or galaxies got involved, I lost interest. He was the one who took on the creation of adventures and characters for the role-playing games that were just beginning to become popular among adolescents, keeping file folders for storylines to explore in *Dungeons & Dragons, Starship Troopers,* and the Western-themed *Boot Hill.* It was Jamie who proved most naturally inclined toward quiet contemplation, whereas I was a child constantly on the move. And even though the dynamic of our differences would change radically as we aged, to the point of having few differences at all beyond degrees of taste, I still think of my brother as having been blessed with the more unique, interesting, and inventive mind. That he only got to produce a fraction of what he was capable of is one of the great injustices I've had the poor fortune to witness, an injustice due in part to his own perfectionism and the ever-growing variety of interests that kept him from focusing on a single project to completion, and due also to the mistaken belief that he had at least an average lifespan over which to pursue his passions. His lasting influence on me, however—in terms of stoking my curiosities, seeking the unfamiliar in order to grasp it, and also as a figure with whom and against whom I came to form my own identity—is irrefutable to my mind and probably a matter for another book.

Still, he never was able to instill in me much fascination for science- or speculative fiction. The only stories of the genre that spoke to me would be, first, the original trilogy of Douglas

Adams's novels, *The Hitchhiker's Guide to the Galaxy,* which overwhelmed my generation of readers as each installment appeared, these small books passed among friends and quoted from, discussed, and debated in depth; and then later, toward the end of high school, Heinlein's *Stranger in a Strange Land,* which struck my young mind as deeply philosophical and only tangentially related to the whole space-trip thing (Valentine, the "stranger" of the title, is a human who was raised on Mars, and is brought to earth, where the rest of the novel remains—a story more involved in cultural critique and our assumptions of the Other than any fantastical speculation that requires bending the space-time continuum). In general, in my own room one would find detective novels and mysteries, comic books, and pop music magazines. Some of my first creative efforts—done in tandem with my brother—involved the creation of comic books, stories in which we invented new heroes and illustrated ourselves.

All this seems normal to me, just part of growing up in a family of readers.

To write "a family of readers" makes us sound more serious and scholarly than we were in reality—a common, mistaken presumption that bugs me about American culture in general: that to read means to be *serious,* or pursuant of the elitist and ignorant-of-"real-life" intellectual life with its rarified tastes, the avoidance of the vulgar (TV), when in honest terms reading was just another way of killing time that wouldn't die, hardly different from going to the movies. Books could be found in any given room. Dad read his thrillers, Le Carré, Ludlum, and "the kind of story where somebody gets killed every few pages," as he liked to put it. Mom read courtroom dramas and loved the medical thrillers by writers such as Sydney Sheldon, and also what she and her friends liked to call their "soft-" or "mom-porn," such as Shirley Conran's *Lace*—a novel my twelve-year-old self surreptitiously read in stolen moments while she was at work or, once I'd located "the good parts," read while she was occupied elsewhere in the house, hypnotized by a narrative that gave me extraordinarily distorted ideas about the sexual world of adults.

No one ever forced us to read. I can't speculate if taking pleasure in books was innate to my brother and me as offspring of two readers, or if it had required heavy persuasion from our parents, any kind of carrot/stick procedure from them, or what. My mother didn't recall how she started us, either; she read to us when we were toddlers, but after that we just seemed to get involved with reading on our own. Likely it helped that we were allowed to read anything we wanted to, always, no matter how basic (comics, and comic strips), or advanced (we competed over who was reading the thickest book, as the width of the spine equated the seriousness of the work in our young heads). Our mother made it seem like an *event*, something *special*, when every two weeks or so the three of us made an outing to the Bon Air branch of the public library, this weirdly planed and angular structure in the Frank Lloyd Wright mold, which I suppose enhanced the allure of books as items of pleasure and entertainment. She allowed us to select as many titles as the library allowed, often expressing her doubts that we could possibly read them all in the two-week allotment of borrowing time, but permitting them to come home with us anyway. Whether we go to them all or not was beside the point; having the books in hand, a stack of them, and my brother and

I showing one another what we had checked out in the car on the way home—him belittling me for yet another Hardy Boys mystery or any other book evidently intended for young age-specific readers; me riding him for his geek interest in the sciences and NASA history—that's what mattered, and what I remember. Collecting was important; keeping hold of an entire series, be it Time/Life books or fictional trilogies. The same with comic books: we each had our specific heroes to collect, and then any offshoot series that branched into its own thing, and dismissed one another's preferences as unavoidably lame. Jamie was a fan of the illustrator Jack Kirby, whose work looked cheap to me. He collected the *Fantastic Four* and *The Incredible Hulk* and *The Silver Surfer*, whereas for me it was *Spider-Man, Daredevil*, and late-period *Captain Marvel* (Mar-Vell, the one with "cosmic awareness"; not the older DC character who shouted "Shazam!"). The only category we could agree on was the obvious superiority of Marvel comics to the DC brand. I speak of the time before the advent of graphic novels, before Batman underwent his dark resurgence and Alan Moore reinvented the genre.

Comic books must have formed some of my first impressions in how stories were told, what was required (beyond the fantastic, heroic elements) to give a narrative its shape and coherence; my first ventures into storytelling consisted of comic books my brother and I created by hand. But it would have to be considered an unconscious influence, as to read Marvel comics analytically was beyond my hurried mind, and it wouldn't have even occurred to me to try to deconstruct an issue of *The Amazing Spider-Man* for the purpose of learning narrative tropes or to study any sort of craft technique, as whatever happened on the page was specific to whoever it was happening to. I was enthralled merely by the stories and the people themselves. Peter Parker, Harry Osborn, Gwen Stacy, Mary Jane, Flash Thompson—these were my friends and guiding lights in growing up.

•

It would be a mistake to imply that reading dominated all other pleasures. As mentioned earlier, though everyone in the family enjoyed reading, to call us a "literary family" would be a grand overstatement. Music inspired lasting reverence. The books and comics were there but music ruled our house. One of my mother's great wishes was to have a quality piano at home, and I remember clearly her excitement and pride the day deliverymen arrived with an upright Baldwin in the driveway, how she hovered over two guys just doing their jobs to insure they did not bump the doorframe on the way in or scratch the dark polished wood as they positioned the instrument in no less than three separate places around the family room until she was satisfied they had found its rightful home—situated against an outside wall perpendicular to the back door and under a window that gave view to nothing but sky when you sat at the bench. Nothing to distract a young boy from the sheet music set before him as he struggled through "The Little Speedboat" and practiced (morosely, once the novelty wore off) the scales and notation his piano teacher demanded he meet over the course of a week. The back door was the most common place of entry to our house, and the piano the first item of interest spotted by anyone who came in. It did not move from its spot against the wall for some thirty years, once my mother recognized she never played it and neither of her sons were interested or able to bring something of the Baldwin's size into their homes.

But in its 1970s heyday, the decade when our parents often hosted parties, there would always be at least one guest who knew his way around the keys, and mother would make a point of having my brother and me sit for a live performance before the adults became too drunk to have us around, the idea being to inspire us toward greater ambition in our own lessons. She desperately wanted us to reach some level of mastery, promising it would bring us great joy once we were older—a joy we could not quite connect to the Van Cliburn albums she put on the turntable at dinnertime, intimate and dexterous music that faded to background behind family chatter and the news on the tiny portable TV. The complexity of the sonatas and concertos on those albums were as easy for my ears to follow as listening to spirited debates in Chinese. Live, though, with the player right there in front of you with hands visible, these brief concerts impressed us with the possibilities—if we could accept the amount of practice required to reach them.

In my case her plan backfired somewhat. If the pianist seemed too impressive, so good as to seem impossibly alien, the unintended effect would be disenchantment, discouragement. It demoralized me to recognize how impossibly far I had to go. To play piano like that, I remember believing back then, you must have to be born to it, a natural. Big hands, long spidering fingers, gave the musician a distinct advantage on the keyboard, and you couldn't compensate for a reach your physiology didn't allow. Rest assured my brother reminded me of this on a regular basis, showing off the number of keys he could span comfortably. I was his physical opposite, built short and broad with small hands, unable to cover an octave. Despite the pleasure of listening to an accomplished pianist produce sounds from the Baldwin that we never heard otherwise, it was dispiriting to see how easy the hands of a graceful adult made it look. How our guest could evoke subtle moods and volumes, whereas even after a couple of years of study my hands seemed to believe that to produce a note I had to smash the key.

There also seemed to be a disconnect between the capabilities of the piano and the music that surrounded us. Mother often proclaimed her love for Van Cliburn and his Rachmaninoff, and at our lessons the teacher might nod to the small plastic busts of Bach and Beethoven and Mozart and Schubert as she demonstrated the different styles of each, but aside from those evenings when Mom wanted to "class up the mood of this place" and tuned the stereo to the classical station or spun one of her LPs (of which there were only two or three, remarkably fewer than the more popular forms we'll get to below), our ears were fed other sounds, other instruments. This was the seventies, the decade when music turned inescapable and ran rampant no matter where you went; it had become a subtle and often not-so-subtle fabric to daily existence, as normal as cars and air. Music wherever you went: shopping in the largest department stores or only popping into the convenience food mart for a gallon of milk; in every office, be it doctor or dentist or school appointment; even the rides in elevators carried a tune. Anywhere you were required to wait, music provided company. There was always a kid with a radio or cassette deck when we organized our games in the street, picking teams for kickball or tag, or the lifeguards at the local pool would have affixed a PA to one of the rock stations. The pianos sometimes heard in these forms of music sounded nothing like the Baldwin that sat under the window in our family room.

•

Silence, however brief, became distinctive and noticeable. Even sleep carried its soundtrack, provided by a small blue globe-shaped transistor radio set on the table beside the bed. In our family we simply did things with music playing, either in the background or as the purpose of conversation: Listen to this. Through our lessons my brother and I were getting our ears trained unknowingly, our brains tweaking to the language of melody and how it worked, the concordance of sounds or its opposite gradually becoming a kind of obsession for me not only in music but later in language of any kind. At our house the classical mode was seldom first choice; it depended on which parent had the floor, as it were. When our father was at work, Mom assumed the controls of the hifi, and we did our chores to a soundtrack provided by The Captain and Tennille, Debby Boone, The Carpenters, Neil Sedaka, and Barry Manilow—a very great deal of Barry Manilow, imprinting in me a susceptibility to sentimental schmaltz and maddening ear worms for which I hold my mother at fault to this day. But when our father came home and he was in the mood, out came the Dylan, Cash, and Waylon—the troubadours you could mention by one name only without worry that whoever was listening wouldn't understand who you meant. Jerry Reed being the anomaly. In his old Cadillac our father kept a perpetual concert going on the eight-track, and it was through his influence and the exposure to that music that interest in the piano began to slip toward oblivion, eventually replaced completely by the instrument that became my lifelong companion: the acoustic guitar.

He had been a folk singer in the sixties covering Dylan, Peter Paul & Mary, and the timeless traditional songs and ballads. His guitar fascinated me even as a child, this old (early 1930s, we've never pinpointed the year exactly) Martin 000–18 with a dark weathered finish and a hairline crack along the soundboard, where the tortoiseshell pick guard had begun to warp. The crack did not affect the sound in any way I could hear, and only enhanced the guitar's magic appeal, gave it its character as something durable, tough, well-crafted—worthy of worship. Though he didn't play as much as he did in the time before having children, anyone paying attention could see the deep satisfaction, this beaming joy that came over him whenever the guitar came out and we started shouting out the songs we wanted to hear. A celebrated bit of family lore has it that he had to be tracked down by my mother's sister the night I was born, that he had to be pulled from the stage of a nightclub where he had been performing in order to greet my arrival.

Many of his songs were essentially stories, and I loved these. The fox and the goose, the long tale of Dylan's "Tangled Up in Blue," and Johnny Cash's renditions of cocaine blues and the woman who wears the long black veil as she wanders the hills and visits her lover's grave in secret—I begged him to play these again and again, often enough that it must have been a relief for him to hand over his guitar for me to play. He showed me the basic chords, positioning my fingers himself, and then declined to teach me more. He knew I wanted a guitar of my own, and said I'd need to prove a committed interest before he would buy one. He gave me a beginner's instruction manual and only allowed me to take the Martin out of its case when he was around, worried my typical clumsy carelessness would damage his prized possession somehow. Once past the basic chords, he said, you can only make real progress on your own. To really learn something, he believed, you have to teach yourself. It's the only way to master a task or craft.

This rule exasperated me for the longest time but I persisted, and eventually came to see the wisdom behind his demand. Rather than being immediately corrected by someone watching, I had to learn to recognize any errors myself, with my own ear, and in this way digested the correction more deeply. The method has an analog in learning to write fiction as well; perhaps it takes longer to recognize missteps on one's own, but once caught, those mistakes are rarely repeated. And like learning the fingering or solo styles of other guitarists, copying the sentences and pace of masters slowly builds confidence and an understanding of how strong sentences and conscious word choice create one's own style of "playing."

It doesn't take very long to master the basics of guitar. Within a few weeks I could move around the frets and change chords with a degree of competence. Despite the usual frustrations of learning anything new, my mistakes were less discouraging than they'd been on the piano, with each difficult chord formation or new scale seen less as a problem and more as a challenge, an opportunity. As with athletics, it seemed I had something of a natural gift, quickly learning a few songs by listening to them on the stereo and figuring their progressions rather than being shown how to play by someone else. My love for the instrument soon overtook my patience with my father's rule that the guitar remain encased when he wasn't around. I practiced whenever I could, wary on the lookout for the sound of his car rolling into our driveway, rushing then to return the guitar to its case in a bedroom closet before he came in through the back door; I'd greet him by asking if I could bring out the instrument now that he was home. It was only a matter of time before my envelopment in the music prevented me from hearing his arrival, though. His discovery got me banned from touching the Martin for a despondent week.

But it also must have convinced him of my dedication to the instrument. Once the ban passed we were in a music shop testing every model that appealed to either of us, but the ones that felt best in my hands were too expensive. He said we would have to wait a while for a proper guitar of my own, and meanwhile I could keep using his, he had no time to play it much anymore anyway. The rule now was that it could never leave the house. Fair enough. I was twelve years old and there was much in the future, especially the next few years, for our family to fight through and suffer, but a triumvirate of solaces had taken shape in me, three centers I could seek whenever in need of an anchor: the soccer ball, the guitar, and books.

Always, it seems, there is something that goes wrong. Whatever he wants, whatever he likes, has sooner or later to be turned into a secret.

—*J. M. Coetzee*, Boyhood

My fourteen-year-old self is distant, more than two-thirds of my lifetime away. I would like to draw on his reading of *A Separate Peace*, to try to access the boy who recognized the novel as the first, perhaps, to truly matter to him—the first to be important to the formation of a writer and even, imperfectly, another self. Appropriating that fresh mind and his reading might illuminate my own more recent encounter with the novel, filtered as it is now by a more mature—or at least older—and writerly mind, a mind with more exposure to and experience in narrative art than the teenaged boy would have imagined as existing. It can be surprising to realize the difference a single text, unchanged in itself over time, can undergo within the same reader.

Retrieving him is difficult, though. That boy's reality emerges only in portions, an instant's flash slowly cohering in detail the way an image gathers on white photo paper steeped in chemicals. Certain specific feelings attach to my memories rather than a clear recollection of events, scenes, who said what and why. I've long envied those people who can recall with any clarity not just moments but entire episodes, great swathes from childhood and adolescence, or at least those who can *believe* that this clarity comes from the facts on the ground as opposed to what their minds have made of it over the years. Perhaps a not-too-perfect memory is helpful in writing fiction, especially if the fiction draws from autobiography; you don't get bogged down with aligning events exactly as they occurred and so feel free to invent from what details you do remember. For my own part such recollections are always sensory, I'll recall the feel of some object in my hand, the timbre of light and length of shadows at a certain time of day, a pungent or fresh odor, maybe one line someone said that struck deep into me. This fourteen-year-old—I can't remember him so much as must try to invent him. The most important thing he owns is his bicycle, a BMX bike comprised of a Red Line frame with Tange TRX forks and the rest of its parts bought separately and pieced together himself. The frame and fork are state-of-the-art for 1982. The frame itself cost an entire summer's wages, and worth every penny. He assists an older boy from his church youth group in a lawn-mowing and landscaping business who pays by purchasing whatever bike part is needed once it has been earned, keeping a tally of hours and amounts on a small yellow pad that slides across the van's dashboard at every turn on the road.

Maybe it's genetic or maybe it's because he's been swimming competitively since he was six or maybe it's due to all the bike riding and lawn care, but the boy is very fit, athletic; he takes home all the first-place ribbons from the annual Field Day at school. This helps make him popular, he's always one of the first to be selected for any team in gym class, almost always surrounded by pals.

At home he has picked up a nickname that pleases and embarrasses him in equal measure: Boy Wonder. Aunt Charlotte, who isn't an actual relation yet is closer to the family than most of those who are related, christened him. She had been listening to his mother proudly recount a weekend's successes in swimming and soccer while both could hear him practicing guitar upstairs—the house's layout makes such sounds inescapable, even when he closes the door and tries to keep the noise down—and both women noted how quickly he was progressing on the instrument, already more proficient than his father, who has played for years. *Boy Wonder Boy Wonder!* she exclaimed, playfully, once he joined them in the kitchen. It would always be expressed twice in quick succession, like a cheer.

He doesn't feel there's anything particularly wondrous about him, but, okay, no reason to make a federal case out of it. A deep source inside him hopes Aunt Charlotte right; maybe there *is* something special in him. He wants to suspect there just might be, if he could ever discover it. Many things interest him and he wants to master them all, but he's found there's always someone else better, someone more advanced in what he hopes to do, to be. Often it feels as though he somehow started at a disadvantage and now must rush to catch up. His special fear is that he'll be found wanting when some unforeseen-but-meaningful moment arrives.

Also he's aware of having quietly collected ample evidence that Charlotte might not think of him so highly if she got to really know him. As in knowing his thoughts. In the past year these have turned aslant, against adults or any figure of authority. He has discovered that by professing obedience and outwardly going along with whatever rules or demands come down from Those Who Rule, he can then go on and do whatever he wants once he's alone. His ethics measured only by evidence. If no one knows he has betrayed their faith in him, then their faith has not been betrayed.

For the past two years his father has been in prison. His mother works long hours to support the family in his absence, and her sons are left with hours of unsupervised and undirected time. On those evenings the so-called Boy Wonder often wanders out to do things he knows he could never explain or admit to unless caught, like hammering nails into the sidewalls of tires, or slipping from house to house to steal all the porch lights on his street, or egging the backs of garages where no one will notice until it begins to smell.

Still, people like him. Typically he likes people, too; an easy friend.

One boy who has known him since fourth grade proposes the idea that they ought to write his biography. They could do it together, print it themselves and bank some coin selling copies to fellow students. It's spring of their first year in high school, an entirely new environment with only a few faces familiar from middle or elementary school. His friend conducts a general poll to scout the market, gauging interest and weighing prices. Pleased with what he discovered, he then makes a real effort at this biography over the course of several days, sitting at the back of class with pencil and notebook in hand while asking probing questions. Where were you born? What did you do before you came to high school? What would you wish people knew about you? Boy Wonder makes an earnest effort to answer every question posed and in sufficient detail, and whatever he could not recall directly he invents on the spot. Yet the more he answers, the more discomfort he feels about the entire endeavor. Part of him doubts the presumptive wisdom of a high school freshman's biography. The usefulness of opening up oneself to mockery. Then a certain question arises during one interview that brings an awkward stop to proceedings: *How would you explain yourself?*

Moments pass without answer. The lack of one and the time passing prove bothersome. He's uncertain why it should be so difficult to find an appropriate response. Is it because the question smacks of parental interrogation, the question his mother might ask after catching him in one of his more bone-headed escapades, like the time he awoke earlier than everyone else and decided to take her car for a tour of the neighborhood? He had congratulated himself for the foresight of evading the busier roads and intersections, and yet still the fearless spree ended with Mrs. Dennison's prized flower beds ruined and one wheel spinning in space above a culvert. But it's not being asked by an angry adult to whom he owes his existence. He scans his classmates, wonders how any of them might answer such a question, or if they could.

Put yourself in that fourteen-year-old boy's shoes. How would you answer? Feel how he freezes in the effort to entertain the question seriously; the project is the idea of a longtime friend and he wants to do well by him and even though he no longer thinks it an especially good idea he figures he could well be wrong, so why not try. He's not against the possibility of making a little extra milk money, and there's a set of chrome alloy bike pedals he's been lusting over for ages. Still, he doesn't know what to explain. How anyone can account for who he is. In quiet moments, when he bothers to look, he doesn't find a particular self to explain; there are his interests, but no explanation for why they interest him. The fact of the matter is he fails to see a why behind what he chooses to do—such as consenting to the idea of a biography, for example, to be covertly duplicated off the ditto machine in the school office—nor does he know why he likes what he likes. He just does.

He worries this line of thinking unveils a failure in himself, a failure *of* himself. That he's marred in some fundamental way. Everyone else, if they have an honest answer to the same question, must be far ahead of him. That nothing is there to explain is disturbing.

His biographer tries to help him out: What rules do you live by, what are your lifetime goals? Boy Wonder realizes he has never thought clearly about these issues. Isn't everyone making it up as they go along? As he stares numbly at his friend's hands resting atop the notepad he performs a rapid mental scan of his interior, a personal inventory in which all the shelves turn up empty. The search continues long enough that it begins to bring forth a discomfort, an unease he senses not only in himself but also, in time, in his biographer. Finally he pleads the innocence of youth: he's fourteen. The rules he lives by are the rules demanded by his parents, unless he can avoid them, and he doesn't have particular goals, maybe he just wants to be happy, he likes to do whatever he finds he likes to do.

His friend nods at his thumbnail scraping the spiral wire along the notebook without writing anything down. Then, rather than following up this abstract philosophical probing with something more particular, he turns curious of his pencil, does the trick of see-sawing it quickly between two pinched fingers so that the wood appears to bend and flex.

Boy Wonder decides there's nothing he likes less than explaining. You can find an explanation for anything you've done or said and and you can even believe it and yet still never know if it was the honest-to-god truth. It might be nothing more than words that sound reasonable; he knows this for a fact, because he's invented plausible reasons to explain his behavior when in trouble any number of times. He knows whenever the adult buys into what he says then whatever he's saying must be the truth.

•

It's an entirely new school and class this year. He's being bused downtown as part of the AP program, and though he believes he is well-liked (no one is spreading rumors about him that he's heard of; nobody has threatened to beat him up), he also feels alone, near lonesome, even, and he wants to hurry and grow up to be an upperclassman like his brother. His brother and his brother's friends all seem to be infinitely cooler, smarter, more clever than he or his friends; they are famous there, having chosen to stay in that school beyond the two years they were required to undergo through busing. These juniors and seniors tolerate him as the tagalong, but he can tell he's not welcome to hang out with them in the smoking section in the parking lot behind the cafeteria where everyone who matters congregates during lunch period. In his class there are few recognizable faces from previous schools.

He makes friends with with Gary Thompson, a boy assigned by his last name to sit in close proximity each morning in homeroom, and a boy who seems as lonesome but appears to be better at accepting it—perhaps because his outcasting is obvious. Gary's from the unfashionable South End of town. He wears a long black nylon trench coat to school even on sunny days with the spring temperatures rising; he wears cheaply made and ill-fitting highwater jeans and bright white Converse canvas sneakers, though he admits his envy for checkered Vans like BW wears. Gary's an odd duck. He even says so, waving off invitations to sit together at lunch with a low-key *No thanks,* and *I'm not trying to be dismissive of you man, it's nothing personal, I'm an odd duck is all.* He says he likes to sit alone at lunch to work on his drawings. Gary is a master of sarcasm and employs it deftly against teachers, bullies, and the pretty girls he knows won't give him the time of day. When he hears of the biography project, it's Gary's withering mockery that leads to the boys coming to their senses and abandoning the venture.

Gary carries a yellow No. 2 pencil behind one ear. His skin has a sallow greenish cast he insists has to do with a drop of mediterranean blood somewhere back in the family tree, and is not indicative of his health. The whites of his brown eyes are always strikingly clear. What the boys have in common, aside from not being terribly interested in listening to teachers droning on from textbooks, is manifold: they both believe landing a job as an FBI or CIA agent would be the height of accomplishment; they've promised one another to apply together after college, once they figure out what's required to join—how come there are never representatives for either agency at the school career fairs? (More proof that the agencies are worth seeking out.) They pass time in classes drawing great military battles on copy paper, soldiers parachuting down atop field artillery and pillboxes, narrowly missing diving planes as they careen through the air or else falling into the rotors of helicopters. Typically the drawings include detailed narratives on the backside explicating the dramas unfolding, stating missions, and the boys trade their compositions back and forth throughout the day while making useful improvements and annotations. Likewise they both are willing to read anything not assigned by class. It's Gary who introduces *The Hitchhiker's Guide to the Galaxy* and the novels following that comprise the trilogy— books to be read when mothers aren't hovering over them to make sure they're doing homework, with quotable lines to toss to one another during the slow periods of the day.

Boy Wonder has ample time without his mother hovering: outside of school, outside of whatever sports practice is in season, he is alone. It's a forced isolation that he's become habituated to, borne by his brother's preference for quiet contemplation, listening to music or reading in his bedroom in the down time before their mother returns from work. BW will read anything, newspapers, grocery lists, cereal boxes, whatever happens to be at hand—but with the warming weather of spring he's drawn out to get on the bike. He owes his freedom to the fact of his father's imprisonment. This presents a conundrum he prefers not to dwell over, though often he finds he's unable not to. He misses his father, and yet it pleases him to have such stretches of time unsupervised, a rarity for boys his age, going by comparison to others in class. No one appears to know how long his father will be away, either; neither of the brothers has been given a clear explanation of what he did wrong, how he got himself into such a shameful situation. They know only that he has been betrayed, double-crossed and slandered by associates he had believed were his friends. Their mother often rails against "the system," vowing to someday write a book she has already entitled *The Other Side of Justice*, an exposé of how anything can be twisted to fit a story for the prosecution.

She tells her sons their father is the victim of his own trusting nature and his ego's sense of invincibility and to let that be a lesson to them. She says he has to pay for playing a small part in a network of good ol' boys and to let that be a lesson too. It's a lesson neither brother understands. They can't even articulate between themselves what the lesson should be. They know only that their father has been transformed into a voice on the telephone for half an hour every Sunday evening, a father for an hour or two once a month when they sit at a table surrounded by all the other fathers-for-an-hour in the prison visiting room, an hour in which he interrogates them for stories about their lives. Both boys are flabbergasted to find themselves suddenly, inexplicably shy at such meetings, without much to tell aside from goals scored, times beaten, books read. There's so much to tell and so much he has missed, they decide, that they can't find a place to begin.

For his part, their father is exploiting his time behind bars to study the bible and find fellowship in Sunday services. Consequently the brothers are more active at church, an Episcopalian diocese, with their mother arranging rides to choir rehearsal, handbells rehearsal and recitals, youth group meetings. She's too busy making a living to drive them herself. The father laments that other men are teaching his sons how to knot a tie, how to shave, the proper mechanics of a handshake. His first-born son learning to drive under the guidance of someone else's father from church. He laments these losses to the boys on the phone and on the extension his wife tells him it should be a lesson for him, she's all about lessons these days since taking over the family business in medical supplies— her, a former elementary school teacher!—and she wants her husband to learn this one lesson real good so when the day comes that he's freed he will never put the four of them into the same position again.

·

Boy Wonder begins to associate his mother with Johnny Carson. Often she's not home until the news just before Carson's show hits the air. She strides in and deposits welcome kisses to both boys and the dog and then quickly banishes the business clothes, the hose and heels, for a nightgown and thick cotton robe. She pours herself four fingers of bourbon to which she adds a trickle of ginger ale, setting the glass on a cork coaster beside her full ashtray, telling her sons she's earned that tall drink and more after another long day the kind of which she hopes they'll never have to understand. She laughs a knowing, low, guttural laugh as Johnny golf-swings through his monologue while she sits cross-legged on her big empty bed surrounded by thick ledgers, invoices, how-to manuals. Often for dinner she picks through leftover french fries gone cold. She tells her youngest son there isn't money to buy him a trench coat like Gary Thompson's and she doesn't have the time to go shopping for one, anyway. The boys are supposed to be in bed by this hour but sometimes she allows them to watch with her for a bit. Though he sees her pull long drafts from her tall glass with deep satisfaction, there seems to be something magic about the drink, as any time he leaves and comes back it looks like nothing has left the glass at all.

One night she calls to tell them she'll be very late and to go ahead and microwave leftover spaghetti for dinner, don't stay up, go to bed when you're supposed to. But even when Carson strides through the heavy curtains to take his place before the camera, she's not there. It's a warm night and his brother has fallen asleep. Boy Wonder decides he's tired of reading and feels up for an adventure. From the fridge and into his backpack goes the styrofoam carton with seven eggs left in it. He slinks out the back door to the garage and hits the night on his bike. It's past midnight by the time he wakes up Gary by scratching his nails back and forth across the bedroom storm screen, a ripping, sinister sound. He's impressed with himself for finding the house, it's a long ride to get there and he doesn't know the neighborhood and has only visited his friend once before. Gary needs intense persuasion before coming outside. He is stuck with only his little sister's bike, too—it lies abandoned in the driveway by the back gate, whereas his own sits in the basement, and liberating it poses too great a risk of waking his parents. Not yet awake enough for sarcasm, Gary bemoans the whole harebrained scheme; he bemoans the sparkling banana seat and colored streamers trailing off the handlebars, bemoans the short cranks engineered for a little girl's legs, it's like he's riding a toy. The entire expdeition is ridiculous, he says, and his father will kill them both when they get caught. Still he comes along.

Boy Wonder has been moved to come here out of concern that his friend needs a lift of the spiritual variety. A bully at his bus stop has forced him painfully low on the food chain and the acceptance of this has gotten Gary down. Nearly every morning at the street corner this mangy bully mocks and intimidates his friend, sometimes beating him up, other times scattering his books and homework, while everyone else waiting for the bus watches and does nothing, too relieved at not being in his place to try to help. It's like he has been made their sacrificial goat, Gary says, a token to placate a beast so the rest can go about their lives unharmed, tilling their fertile lands and expecting a bountiful harvest. He doesn't know why the guy has focused on him and says it doesn't matter. Maybe it's the pencil that bothers him, the guy is always pulling it from behind Gary's ear and snapping it in two a few inches before his face. One time an older girl tried to help out, telling the guy he wasn't proving anything or impressing anyone by beating on Gary, and the bully responded by yanking her purse from her shoulder and throwing it on the ground and pissing on it. The guy pissed on this girl's purse, can you believe that?

The remnant of his pencil was helpful that day, allowing them to pick up her purse by the strap without touching it.

Gary can't fight. He just can't. His fists are inept. So most days begin with his humiliation. It is precisely the sort of injustice Boy Wonder, a committed adherent to the moral order put forth in Marvel Comics, cannot allow to stand. . . . He tells Gary he wants to see the house where this bully lives; he says he wants to see what kind of car the father drives. Gary clarifies that the bully and his brother live with their mother only, there's no father around, in fact if he wasn't always beating him he might even feel kind of sorry for the guy.

Boy Wonder states that lacking a father doesn't give you the right to be an asshole. He doesn't say he feels himself to be proof of this; he hopes Gary will point it out on his own. He refuses to let it bother him when his friend fails to come through as hoped, and reiterates instead that they'll check out what the brother drives, then.

The lights of the house are off. A station wagon sits in the driveway before the closed garage door. How bad can the brother be if he drives a station wagon? Boy Wonder eases the book bag off his shoulder and shows Gary what he's brought along. He presents one perfect egg naked in his outstretched palm. He asks his friend what they should do.

I'm not doing anything, Gary tells him. What's more, Gary clarifies, he wants to put on the record here that this idea is one of his friend's stupider ones.

You'll feel better.

I won't, says Gary. Or more exactly I will, but only until this guy figures out I am here tonight, after which I'll suffer a great deal of physical and psychic pain.

Boy Wonder shrugs, makes as though he's going to return the egg to its box. Then he cackles, and quickly hurls it from where they stand straddling their bikes on the street, watching the egg sail in an arc over the easement, the sidewalk, the short rise of the front yard, to splatter against the bricks beside the double front window. Immediately the two are off. Gary, bare-foot and struggling with the short cranks designed for a young girl, has to work hard to catch up to where BW waits at the very corner where the humiliations occur so many mornings.

Revenge is sweet, he tells his friend. Isn't it? And Gary admits this whole thing is kind of thrilling. So now it's your turn, Boy Wonder says. You'll feel so much better, it'll be like you landed a good punch to his nose.

He requires a great deal of convincing and assurances but it's not long before Gary has set his sister's bike down at the edge of the street before his enemy's home, each hand clutching an egg. He admits in a whisper how ill-advised this feels. BW whispers back that tomorrow he'll be at the bus stop listening to his nemesis complain about what somebody did to his house and if Gary can just keep himself quiet and not smile, he'll get to enjoy at least a small taste of revenge.

Six eggs left. The plan is for each to throw three and then take off in different directions. Take off at first sight of a light flicked on inside, or any movement at the front door.

They're in the middle of the plan's execution when confronted by an unexpected development: not everyone was home for the night. The older brother doesn't drive a station wagon, he drives a refurbished 280Z and works second shift at the aluminum plant and his headlights surprise the boys in mid-throw. They take off, but, as before, Gary's bare feet and short cranks make him slow out of the gate. The older brother is fast on his feet. Boy Wonder is away and off into the dark when he hears Gary's bike go down on the pavement. Still he heaves ahead at full speed, dodging the bells of streetlight glow as best he can, not stopping until he reaches a dead end where the suburb stops at a black stand of trees next to some farmer's field. He stands there in the shadows and guilty, quiet, looks back from where he's come and tries to decide what to do.

He imagines he can hear distant screams.

Soon the waiting without sign of his friend becomes too much. In the end he doesn't make a rational decision to return so much as, once he's regained his breath and remounted the bike, his pedals take him back to the scene. It's brilliantly lit now, the house lights on and the front door open to a bright room inside, the doorway framing an older woman in a robe who stands cross-armed and tousle-headed; the headlights of the 280Z cross the front yard and illuminate the house and beads of dew stand out in precise detail on the grass. A police cruiser spotlights the rest, the girl's bike on its side in the street where it fell, its limp candy streamers sparkling.

·

For his honesty in returning unprompted and for insisting to the police and Gary's father that the entire episode was his own idea and not Gary's, Boy Wonder wins a free ride home without arrest. He's surprised how the fact of Gary's sufferings at the hands of someone in the egged household does not extend any validity or sympathy to the cause. On the drive home the officer asks what had he been thinking and Boy Wonder admits he hadn't been thinking at all, it was like he was living in some story and going through the motions of what he had been scripted to do. The officer tells him to find a better explanation for when he tells his father what he did. Boy Wonder explains he won't have to tell his father, at least not for a few days, and explains why. The officer, who seems like a nice man despite his pencil mustache and the toothpick rolling from side to side in his mouth, tells him he should plan better next time, and not get caught.

At home his mother rages fuming at the front door. Before the officer has the bike out of the trunk and can explain what her son has done that brings him home in a police car, she has her grip on the boy's ear and twists it just like they do in a Three Stooges skit, doubling the boy over. She tells the officer to please come in for a moment and wait while she takes care of her son, shouting as she continues her hold up the stairs, What did you do? What did you do? and marching him into his bedroom, hesitating long enough only to slap him hard across the face when he turns to mouth meaningless apologies.

•

Gary does not appear in class the next day. When Boy Wonder returns home he finds a padlock attached to his bedroom door and its frame. His brother apologizes for what he has been instructed to do, but doesn't feel so badly that he can resist teasing him for how stupid he has been. Neither know for how many nights he is to be a prisoner. Their mother, still at work, isn't around to ask. He is supposed to take this opportunity to do homework, and, recognizing this, his first thought is to rebel, pick up his guitar in protest and refuse to do anything but play until the calluses on his fingers bled—and at this moment he notices the guitar gone, the fine molded case no longer lying on its side at the foot of his bed.

She really knows how to punish, his mother. She has a gift, really thinks things through. He's furious at his predicament even as he respects it as earned. He broods over the options of somehow denying her satisfaction, how he might make her pay somehow, what could he imagine doing to bring her regret. Nothing comes to mind immediately. It's small room, only enough space for his desk and the bed pushed to the wall below the window, a window he can crawl through if need be, the drop to the ground isn't high. In this frame of mind he picks up the slim novel assigned for English class, entitled *A Separate Peace*. He's not sure what the title means. Even after reading the summary and praise on the back cover he doesn't understand what it means.

Here's an opportunity, however frail, to prove his resistance; here's something he can readily hate. The book helps him out by beginning slowly. He doesn't want to like it, by nature he tends to dislike anything not discovered on his own, anything he's required to engage with, and feels it his special duty to dislike and resist anything imposed on him while a prisoner. An unnamed narrator is relating his return to a private school fifteen years after being a teenaged student there during the Second World War. It doesn't seem like much is happening, either, as for some reason the narrator visits the marble stairs of the First Academy Building and then walks through wet grass and November cold to locate a tree beside a river. None of the narrator's actions or thoughts mean anything to the reader and three pages in he is beginning to wonder already if *CliffsNotes* are available for this book so he wouldn't have to suffer throughout the entire actual story until its end. He wonders if his mother, the situation between them being what it is, would even allow him to buy *CliffsNotes* for studying.

But then there comes a peculiar statement that piques his interest, a hint of what might be coming: *Nothing endures, not a tree, not love, not even a death by violence.* The sentence captures the mood its reader has found himself to, a melancholy frustration, even as he's aware he does not quite understand the full ramifications of what is being said or what it means in this context. The promise of some violence usually bodes well for any story, but what could be more enduring than a death by such violence, or any death for that matter? He 's curious to know. The phrase "nothing endures" articulates a truth he has suspected for a time without putting into words; a statement of how he feels since his father left to serve out his prison sentence, the two words pungent with both positive and negative connotations. The positive: his father will not be in prison forever. In the future there exists a day, exact date unknown at this time, when his father will return. The negative: he never realized, growing up, how fragile a thing like family could be; his place as the youngest part in a four-square group had felt timeless, permanent, a bald fact of living, and never had he felt the slightest suspicion that this reality was composed of numbered days—a finite number silently counting down to its final end. To zero. If he had known that in advance, surely he would have appreciated his time more. He would have been more fully present, more deeply engaged in his own life. He would have paid attention.

Phineas appears, one from a group of boys mulling about the base of a tree. Something about him brings an immediate sense of recognition, the presence of a fellow traveler. This in spite of the old and out-of-fashion slang he speaks; no teenager in 1983 would use the phrase "a cinch" regarding some kind of physical challenge such as climbing the great tree in the story, nor would one wonder, as narrator Gene does, whether a friend had gone "completely goofy." Nobody talks like that anymore and it's hard for him to believe the generation of World War II soldiers did; in his imagination those men were too tough and heroic to sound so square. The bits of dialogue make the boys in the novel seem younger, more sheltered than they were supposed to be, like a couple of kids out of *Leave It to Beaver*.

Still it makes sense that the presence of a great tree over-looking a river, in summer, required the boys to climb it. Trees existed in order to be climbed. The daring to step out on one unsteady branch and leap into the water is just a bonus—the threat of falling before making the river's edge being what made the challenge worthwhile. He understands too Phineas's reasoning, that if he proves he has the wherewithal to jump from tree to river, then everyone there had to do the same. It only makes sense. Just outside his own bedroom window stands a great maple that had taught him to climb—him and and his brother and everyone else in the neighborhood. He had been proud to be the one willing to climb highest, to where the branches turned stripling-weak. They had made a game of it, he and the other boys, attaching masking tape to the highest point as proof of how far one had reached. And he's aware of the danger the tree possesses, too: some years before he had broken his wrist while playing war, his sniper posi-tion discovered by his brother, who shot at him from below. Caught up in his imagination to play his death realistically, Boy Wonder dropped through the branches without care until his arm snapped against the ground. This feat had earned him worry and ire from his parents, eye-rolling from his brother, and respectful renown from the other boys on his street.

He doesn't read of Phineas so much as it feels like he is getting to know him, becoming acquainted with a new friend who has entered his life unexpectedly. The more he reads, the more he comes to appreciate what the boy says and does, an instant agreement between them and no explanations needed.

He understands him easily, and for the first time begins to dwell over the fact that he has come to identify so closely with a person who doesn't exist—a person made from words on paper—and yet still he interprets the boy as a proper reflection of himself; if not a perfect reflection, perhaps, then an idealized one. A perfected facet of his person. First the unusual name, Phineas, a name he has never heard before, which imparts a degree of the exotic in his mind along with identification. He, too, had been given a singular name—Kirkby, a family name, his English (Leicester) grandmother's maiden name—one that he hates, and for many years has wished he could change, though now in high school he is beginning to appreciate the tacit way it sets him apart from the Garys and Joes and Scotts and Gregs of his world. Still, he wishes he could change it to something less unusual and precious. But for Phineas the name is only the first emblem of his singularity. What matters is what the boy does, the way he acts. Boy Wonder is quickly enthralled by the audacity of his actions, his willingness to take chances, his exemplary faith in himself, his honest willingness to do good on behalf of his friends. Especially his best friend Gene, the one who was evidently moved to write about him. His ability to spout nonsense to deflect trouble from authority, and even his accepting-but-indifferent attitude to the adults in charge of Devon:

> Phineas didn't really dislike . . . authority in general, but just considered authority the necessary evil against which happiness was achieved by reaction, the backboard which returned all the insults he threw at it.

Yes, that's exactly what it's like, although he never would have expressed it in quite the same way, not even if someone— his friend Gary, for example—had asked him. Halfway through the book it feels as though its author, John Knowles, had some- how inhabited this reader's mind and understood how to bring language to feelings and assumptions that the almost-fifteen- year-old boy held without even knowing. What a gift, to be able to do that! How did he accomplish such a thing?

As he reads on he begins to detect similarities in the friendship between the two boys and his own friendship with Gary, whose fate is still unknown. Himself as Phineas of course, Gary as Gene. Phineas spouting nonsense theories to account for the enigmatic pink shirt, or the reason he wore the school tie as a belt—these had exact corollaries in Boy Wonder's own life; a pink oxford had been selected as the uniform for his church handbell choir (pink shirt, gray slacks), and though the boys had rebelled at first they settled on only voicing complaint, there had been talk of organizing a strike to make the point, yet in the end each knew it was a losing battle, the outfits had been purchased already after all. Eventually they came around to the idea with grudging acceptance. Since then he has taken to even wearing the shirt to school, readily firing back at the inevitable teasing from other boys on the bus while basking in the appreciation expressed by more than one girl.

There is Phineas's self-confident nonchalance, the way he goes about breaking the school record for the 100 Yards Free Style, just to see if he could do it. The same event is his own specialty on the swim team. There is Phineas talking Gene into risking expulsion to set off on an expedition to a faraway beach on their bikes, riding for hours to set their feet in the ocean, and he can easily envision himself corralling Gary Thompson again (on a proper bike, this time, and not his little sister's) to skip school and ride maybe to the backside of Churchill Downs in order to wander among the horses, or else maybe to the waterfront, where he suspects there are a number of challenging trails—once from the bridge he'd caught glimpses of them through the thin trees while riding with his mother back from Indiana. Phineas and Gene spend the night on the beach and there isn't an analogous corollary in the real world of Louisville, but the idea of sleeping in the open on a beach is a possibility he stamps into his memory, an experience he will seek once he has a car and is as free as this Phinease kid in the book. The closest he can get to it now would be to spend the night in those same woods with the trails which are known to harbor hobo camps due to its proximity to the rail lines. Now that held the promise of real adventure. But even with having earned the nickname Boy Wonder, he admits to himself (reluctantly) that he isn't so carefree or brave enough to hazard such a risky adventure as that.

He has never been to New England. He knows next to nothing about the region save the names of its NFL teams. The Devon school is private, a prep school (the meaning of which he has to look up), a type of place he knows nothing about—did such places still exist? and why? why would parents send their sons away to grow up without them?—and he assumes such schools must be a misery to attend, since they lacked girls. Despite these foreign details the novel still feels as real to him as his own life. This Knowles guy captures perfectly the feeling of summer and its freedoms and how it feels to be a teenager without adults around to bother anybody.

The greatest difference between the novel and his life is the presence of World War II. Even on his first reading he understands how the war colors everything for the boys, it exerts pressure on every thought, every decision, how it positions a bracing melancholy to the story as a whole; without the pressure of their entire world engaging in war, and the boys' certainty that their futures are inescapably bound up in it, he cannot imagine exactly what sort of story the book would have. Whether he would still find the novel so engrossing. The fact of the war awaiting them gives the boys' lives their vitality and meaning; even the existence of the great tree from which they jump is associated with war, as part of an obstacle course the seniors use for training in preparation for the military; the title of the book stands out only in reflection of the distant war raging about their world.

His life feels so weightless in comparison. He knows he should be grateful for not having a war awaiting his arrival. Yet he wonders if his own life is missing an essential ingredient, a noble challenge against or within which he would be defined, a calling he would be required to meet or else face a life of shame and self-hatred.

There's no overt war to make such demands to boys his age. Instead there exists a tension he chooses not to ignore: no outright war but the teeming threat of one, this simmering mood called the cold war that he discusses with his brother often. Any teenaged male who bothered to pay attention to news beyond the sports page could be forgiven for wanting to get in some kicks now, before he ended up in a cockpit or behind a rifle. A few months before, in the late fall, the US had invaded tiny Grenada, an island nation in the

Caribbean nobody had ever heard of nor, as far as he could tell, did anyone understand why the military bothered with such an insignificant place. His brother, grimly knowing as usual, described it as practice. Practice for what evidently lay in store either sooner or later, as suggested by the bombing of marine barracks in Beirut not even two weeks later, a tragic hit in which some 300 servicemen lost their lives. The Soviets were shooting down civilian airlines for no apparent reason. Their father, a veteran, had instructed them to keep an eye on the problems in El Salvador and Central America in general, because "those twists in Washington" would get boys on the ground there eventually, just wait and see.

It made sense to learn what you could. Try not to worry and yet be prepared. Both brothers had come to follow world events in childhood, their earliest memories filled by astronauts on the moon and images of Vietnam's jungle war played out on the TV every night. They were the only kids in the neighborhood who could point to Cambodia on a map and explain the word *genocide*. Since fifth grade he had begun writing letters of support and advice to then-President Carter, who even a child could see needed a helping hand. And then he had become riveted by the supreme suspenseful drama of the long crisis in Iran, where US citizens were held hostage by—this detail was difficult to get his head around—*students*. He followed the coverage closely in the two newspapers that arrived at home (this was an age in which newspapers offered detailed analysis, when articles used language that required proximity to a good dictionary and were not written to a grade-school level for readers who couldn't be expected to strain their attention beyond a handful of column inches), the

Courier-Journal in the morning and the *Louisville Times* in the evening. The hostage crisis kind of became his thing, what he became known for in middle school, like he was the school's correspondent for world affairs. He took clippings from both papers to present in the weekly Current Events module in which each student addressed the class on news of the day.

He doesn't know why the hostage crisis had sustained such a peculiar fascination for him. Perhaps because of his imprisoned father, a hostage of a different sort. He read the stories about negotiations, read the mini-biographies of each hostage that began to appear in batches of two or three over those 444 days; became fascinated by how an entire life could be boiled down to a series of essential details; learned why these students hated their Shah and, by extension since they were giving him refuge, the United States. He stared at pictures of blindfolded Americans with hands bound behind their backs corralled by dark men with heavy beards, and wondered what it must be like to be there under the blindfold, to be at the mercy of angry strangers who did not speak your language. Were they bound and blindfolded all the time? Were they all kept within the same room? What did they do all day—what did they do when they needed to go to the bathroom?

What would he be like, if he found himself in the same situation?

He had fantasized ways he would have led his fellow captives to escape; each plan required a great deal of Iranian blood, and of course not everyone would get out alive. He remembers the weight of sorrow that had unnerved him when recounting to the class the failed rescue mission called Operation Eagle Claw. It meant something dire to him, accounting for their nation's failure—an impossibility, for they were the good guys and justice should always prevail—to his fellow classmates, even though the details made for a thrilling story like something out of a movie. A movie with the wrong ending. President Carter had approved a mission in which eight helicopters left a carrier in the gulf to reconnoiter at a desolate staging area in Iran's desert. They flew swiftly through moonless night and under complete radio silence. Immediate obstacles assailed them: a massive, damaging dust storm swept over the aircraft, narrowing the force to five working helicopters for an operation planned to have at least six. The commanders waited for word from the president over how to proceed, passing hours in enemy territory until the authorization came down to abort the mission—and the story should have ended there, with our boys retreating now to fight another day, and nobody the wiser: a mission kept so secret, it had never happened. Except the staging area's evacuation became a debacle when one helicopter crashed into a plane heavy with fuel, resulting in an explosion that killed eight US soldiers and lit up radars across the Middle East.

The news made for a terrible embarrassment to the US in general and to President Carter in particular, a failure felt even by an eleven-year-old boy in Kentucky. He did not want to accept that his country had failed in what should have been a thrilling act of heroism—for that's what those men were, he thought: real honest to goodness heroes. His father had been an Army Ranger trained for such all-action missions, ready to carry out silent and secretive killings of the enemy, unafraid to engage in hand-to-hand combat. At times he thought maybe, possibly, he might join the Delta Force himself when he grew old enough. (Once, while watching some patriotic adventure movie on TV, his father had laughed at a scene where rangers snuck up on an enemy guard, clasped his forehead, and ran a blade across his throat. "That's a bunch of nonsense! They didn't train us to do that at all," he said, getting up from the couch. "Open a man's throat and you'll be surrounded before the body drops. All that air bellowing out of the lungs makes all kinds of noise. Come here"—and here he moved behind his son and grasped the hair on his crown—"See, what you do is the exact opposite, you push the head down and drive your blade in at the base of the skull. Like how you pith a frog in school. You've never pithed a frog? Well, you're not there yet. You'll see what I mean in a couple of years.")

The fantasy had slipped tentative hooks into him, this notion of training as a paratrooper, an Army Ranger (after all, wasn't he a natural athlete himself, perfect for such exercises?) prepared to take on the USSR when that inevitable day arrived. In movies it looked like there was nothing more noble or worthy of honor. But he paid attention, growing up, smart enough to slowly mark the great differences between movies and the news. For as long as he could remember there was a small TV set on the kitchen counter which showed the news during dinnertime, and his earliest memories of what he had seen there were jungle and beach images from the failure in Vietnam, and then the failure in the Iranian desert, and then the more recent bombing of the barracks in Beirut. He has started to suspect the military of being dangerously incompetent, not worth trading his life for. They needed to get their act together, he and his brother agreed.

Now the Soviets—the "Evil Empire," he'd learned from President Reagan—are stirring hell in Afghanistan, and this is very much on his mind (and the TV). As is his country's recent deployment of Pershing missiles in West Germany. And just that month the US had provoked the Evil Empire into some serious bluster, breaching Soviet airspace while conducting Navy exercises in the North Pacific. To listen to the talk on that small TV or the radio in his mother's car, war, perhaps even nuclear war, awaited just beyond the horizon—probably around the time he reaches the proper age for a draft. His mother had suggested this to him once, and sadly. She had been looking him over with a kind of marveling astonishment, this strange mood she fell into from time to time, as though she couldn't quite believe in the physical fact of either son, the miracles of their arms and legs, their ten fingers and toes. She doesn't want either of her boys to be soldiers.

Twice a semester in every year of school the teachers directed their classes through disaster drills, preparation for fire, tornadoes, and bombs. Always he had followed the instructions dutifully. But ever since the time another seventh grader quietly voiced his own reservations about the worth of these procedures, he has wondered if curling up with face tucked against knees, hands clasped behind head, would make any difference to Armageddon. Gary Thompson agreed: they'd be goners. The interior walls framing the school's courtyard are made entirely of glass, and it's easy to imagine the windows bursting into millions of shards to shred the little bodies of students snuggled up below their lockers.

The issue simmers in his mind more trenchantly than is likely healthy. Knowles recognizes this anxiety, speaks to it early on in the novel, in the opening section. There, the adult Gene seeks out places he recognizes from his time as a student:

Preserved along with it, like stale air in an unopened room, was the well-known fear which had surrounded and filled those days, so much of it that I hadn't even known it was there. Because, unfamiliar with the absence of fear and what that was like, I had not been able to identify its presence.

He wouldn't identify it precisely as fear, if he'd been asked, but more as a kind of constant worry, a preoccupation he has made conscious effort not to dwell upon in those moments when he was most susceptible: the time alone, in bed, trying to sleep, or that long hour drowsing on the public bus that brought him home from downtown late in the day after swim practice. Should he call it fear? The feeling is more like morbid fascination, a fearsome stirring in his imagination. Many times he would be resting on the bus with his head lolling against a window, the engine vibrating the glass and into his skull, and through half-closed eyes he might picture a missile's sudden impact, right in the middle of an intersection. There would be a brief high screaming narrowing in from above, and as people looked up to find its origin they would be engulfed in a blinding flash, an explosion so fierce as to deafen the few who weren't killed outright. Yes, everybody gone deaf save perhaps a ringing in the ears. And he would imagine what that scene would look like, how strange it would feel to watch in that queer silence, all senses stunned by the explosion, as panic broke out among the bus passengers and hysteria overtook the streets. . . . Boredom and fatigue gave rise to the worst scenarios in him. Is that the kind of fear that the adult Gene was talking about? Or is it an effect of too many movies seen acting on some nihilistic bend in his head? Did it mean something is wrong with him?

Regardless, he believes he understands what the author means: a fear like a low-grade fever so consistent and thorough and unavoidable that you are hardly aware it's there, it permeates the very stuff of reality. Only once it has disappeared could you identify its existence. Despite the war around them, the boys in the book, he believes, are actually more innocent of worldly fears than he has had to be, for the fears that have welcomed him, the ones that have been forming him without his knowledge, weren't created until those boys were adults. Despite the looming distant war their summer can be seen as a true idyll, an actual Eden, living in an era in which genocide and nuclear war mean nothing. Phineas and Gene have never laid eyes on scenes of burning bodies, mushroom clouds; they never heard the famous speech at the United Nations in which Khrushchev beat his shoe on the dais as he proclaimed "We will bury you!"

The adult Gene, however, *does* possess such knowledge. Against such knowledge Gene can rebuild that idyllic summer of 1942. He can be forgiven for making the most of their innocence almost to the point of making the boys too incredible for a reading boy to believe. Knowles must have expected readers of successive generations to recognize this, and conceived his novel accordingly.

What adds to the simmering anxiety in his own mind is his own innocence; this he can identify himself. He's never been able to formulate an understanding Why behind the Cold War, the tensions between the Evil Empire and the Great Society. Nor has he discovered a reasoning Why either government has bothered to prepare itself with armories powerful enough to annihilate not only their perceived enemy but all life on the planet several times over. A line in the novel speaks to him in this regard, comforting to frail extent in that it clarifies his confusions as not specifically relevant to the age in which he lives or even to the generation in power, but to the mere fact of being human: "It seemed clear that wars were not made by generations and their special stupidities," Gene says, "but that wars were made instead by something ignorant in the human heart." Something else to ponder on those achingly long bus rides home, another assertion to daydream-wander through, a line of inquiry directed toward the discovery of what that ignorant something actually is. An inquiry that requires, he soon comes to realize, that he write his thoughts in order to pursue them.

·

Phineas accepts his athletic gifts as normal, natural, inseparable from who he is. Breaking a longstanding school record, excelling at most any sport despite not being of heroic size— Finny on the page can't imagine his self separate from these characteristics, and the same holds as well to the boy reading him. He identifies so thoroughly with the boy who initiates the Super Suicide Society of the Summer Session that it feels like he may as well be reading about himself; a slightly different, best self, transposed into a different time. Meaning: what he would have been like had he been born a few decades earlier. Rather than being astounded by Finny's peculiar perfection, which some in class call unrealistic, he has a rapport with all that Finny does and says. Finny just makes sense in his conception of how things are, and it makes perfect sense that for such a natural human being a shattered leg goes far beyond the mere pain of physical injury; it is a harrowing, unwanted change in personhood. For an athlete to lose the ability to play, to engage in any strenuous physical activity at all, goes beyond frustrated disappointment—he suffers a personal diminishment; his own understanding of self, of purpose, perhaps even his meaning is undone.

In this regard the novel presents him with more than an engaging story. Rather it becomes a terrifying tour of the possibilities—akin to the journeys Scrooge takes on a single Christmas Eve in the company of the ghosts of Christmas past, present, and future; a look at all that could go wrong in his own life, if he were to become unlucky. The possibility of a maiming injury that could keep him from the soccer fields, the trees to climb, the beloved Redline bike with its rad mag wheels, meant the loss of joys that anchor him, that give his own being its shape. It annoys him that after the fall from the tree the novel pulls away from Finny to focus almost exclusively on the narrator Gene. He wants to get back to Finny's misfortune, not dwell on Gene's guilty ramblings. Through Finny he weighs the same fears that come in quiet nighttime moments when the world's worries arrive and his thoughts turn morbid. He recognized early in the reading that the story was going to be a sad one, and he's read enough to have formed the opinion that all the really good stories are, but still he holds hope that the sadness in *A Separate Peace* will be offset by Finny's recovery.

Thoroughbreds are made for running and nothing else. If the horse suffers an injury that prevents its ability to run, the accepted wisdom is to save the animal from its misery and put it down. A human athlete can't be put down like that, obviously, but he believes the horse's fate makes a good analogy for what he might become if he were to suffer the same. In this light Phineas becomes a model to learn from if the unthinkable were to happen. Admirably Phineas appears to be made of brave stock and eschews bitterness, refuses to wallow in the easy welcome of anguish, lacks even the capacity, it seems, to blame his friend for the accident. Instead he transfers his interests and ambitions to Gene, who accepts them out of guilt or that fear he mentioned, it's unclear which. It might even be for the love of a best friend trying to make amends. Actually it's surprising to see how well the boy on the page adapts to this cruel turn; he's unsure how he would take any similar suffering himself. The so-called Boy Wonder half-imagines himself ripe for a tragic experience of his own—his parents have often chided him for his recklessness in games, a midfielder who dives into tackles with free abandon, a relatively small player unafraid to bang against older, stronger, larger boys. A little pit bull on the pitch, according to his high school coach. He had broken four bones by the time he turned twelve, each sustained while having fun.

I did not know everything there was to know about myself, and knew that I did not know it, Gene writes. These words sink in deeply, words as true as anything he knows for certain, as true and certain as his father's love. And more:

> I alone was a dream, a figment which had never really touched anything. I felt that I was not, never had been and never would be a living part of this overpoweringly solid and deeply meaningful world around me.

These lines do not strike their proper resonance until the second reading, once he has grasped the entire story and becomes more forgiving and patient with Gene, even halfway interested in him as he tries to distinguish Gene's motivations and possible culpability, the whole mystery of intent behind the jouncing of the tree limb.

The initial reading passed quickly over two nights while he hungered to know what happened next, and then what after that, and again until he made it to the end, the final passage that he gathered as a kind of wisdom but, unfortunately, the meaning of which he found perplexing and inscrutable. No sooner has he finished the novel than he does something he has never done before: he returns to page one and starts over again. Second readings—and often a third and fourth—will become an acquired habit in the years that follow, a rule he will hold to the point that he comes to consider a book read once as a book still unread. Yet when he returns to the beginning this first time he feels like he's getting away with something, like he's cheating somehow.

He's not exactly sure why he's reading it again, either; he knows what's going to happen, after all. Reruns of shows he's seen on TV never interest him. Something inside him, however, isn't ready to leave this novel behind just yet. Maybe it's an urge to better understand the work as a whole, while his mind still holds some of what his teacher had said about it during class discussion, or because he feels a pull to re-inhabit the world written there, a familiar, melancholy world that reflects his own mood from being locked into his bedroom every evening. Soon he will seek that world and find in it a kind of harbor, he will pursue moments in which book and boy are especially attuned to one another. The second reading reveals the hand of the artist at work, prompting a deeper appreciation of the decisions made in selecting the order of action, and which details to use and underscore—he congratulates himself for noticing Knowles's emphasis on the First Academy building and its marble steps in the opening pages, for instance; details that didn't register with him the first time through. And although he still resists Gene he comes to sympathize with his predicament, his sense of guilt and awkward longing.

For in the days to come he too is fated to greet extensive misfortune. The "overpoweringly solid world" reasserts itself, and like Gene he will feel he is no living part of it, adrift, without real form, and meaning little. Another fear seeded, one more fear to grow and twine through all the others that will constitute his personal struggle for the rest of his life. It's no more than a week after his class finishes the novel. Everyone has turned in their papers and the teacher has begun to introduce them to this concept called existentialism, preparing the grounds on which they'll approach Albert Camus and *The Plague*. Still his mind dwells over the two boys at school during the war, still turning over what might have been different for Phineas, and the question of Gene's guilt, whether Gene intended the accident to happen or not. It's later that afternoon when the solid world leaves Boy Wonder writhing from a grave injury of his own.

Notwithstanding the punishment at home and his imprisonment in his bedroom, his mother allows him to continue in school activities like the soccer team, as a lesson in keeping commitments. A lesson she rationalized after the fact; his brother's insistence that even though only a freshman he was considered an integral cog in the team's machine had helped her to this conclusion. He's normal-sized for his age and thus small against the boys about to graduate, but he has a solid build and explosive speed, enough to get him named to the varsity lineup. That day he had already played the JV game beforehand but didn't feel tired in the least, more like his body was in its best form. Early in the second half he's charging with the ball across the penalty area, two big defenders tight on his heels, and with an extra step he creates just enough space to turn, shoot, and then take the collision he knows is coming. Already turned sideways and in the air, the impact sends him spinning and into an awkward fall: his knee spikes the ground hard enough to pop out the head of his femur from its socket, and then the hip slams down next with all the weight of his body and momentum, jamming the head back into place and shattering the right side of his pelvis.

The kind of collision that happens countless times in any game of soccer, but in this case one that produces pain unlike any he could imagine to suffer. A pain of such intensity as to render him incapable of straightening out his body for the trainers to examine him, nor can he do it for the paramedics once they arrive in their ambulance, the shock causing a kind of rigid paralysis that leaves him stuck in a twisted, fetal-like position, legs folded over one another. They bring him like that to the hospital. Only after several shots of lidocaine and a soothing IV drip do the muscles relax enough for the x-rays, and he gazes in dismay at the ghostly white fluorescence of his body's interior and sees the damage there: rivering cracks spread out and cross over one another in angry lines from the socket all the way to the edge of what he learns is called the iliac crest, to where bright white bone fades to a muted, milky blue. The doctor explains that these murky areas show where his pelvis has yet to harden completely; his skeleton, he's surprised to hear, isn't yet all bone; everywhere there are these cartilagenous areas that won't harden until he is fully a man.

The doctor expresses concern: he can't be certain the breaks haven't reached into these soft places. The severity of the damage would change significantly if so—the injury might never fully heal, or possibly the patient will be maimed, prone to further injuries, a lopsided walking gait. No more sports.

He can no longer trust his own body; his own body has betrayed him. It has always felt invincible. Even the previous broken wrists, the cracked collarbone, the sprained ankles, were merely brief setbacks along the path of growing up rambunctious and wild, and each had healed quickly. He'd never swallowed a painkiller before. He had never stayed in the hospital before, either, but because the doctors decide against wrapping his body in a cast, they keep him there for ten days. The medicine makes him sleepy, slow-minded, thirsty. His body no longer feels the need to go to the bathroom, and by the third day he finds this profoundly disturbing, wondering where all his waste is getting stored and for how long could it stay there. Some nights his mother sleeps in the room with him and his brother stays with a neighbor. While he watches her sleep he feels a gnawing inside, a dawning guilt for how he has tried her during his father's absence, how he has angered and frustrated her, betrayed her trust. He wants to apologize. Sincerely apologize. But he doesn't know how to lead her into a conversation in which his apology would feel appropriate and honestly sincere. In those sleepless nighttime hours, in the hospital's near-quiet punctuated by ringing phones and chiming machines, the steely clack of beds on wheels, he begins feeling—very much so—like the child he is again.

He misses his father. The situation wouldn't be so bad if he could pick up the phone and call him, wake him in the middle of the night so he'll know his youngest son can't sleep even on painkillers. Maybe the father doesn't sleep so well, either, and so ringing him up would make for a welcome respite from staring blankly at the ceiling. They should allow telephones in prisoners' cells, he decides. It's not like his father killed anybody.

There are visitors. The first is the teacher of his AP English class, Mr. Jarboe, who arrives with homework "as a favor," so he won't fall too far behind. Jarboe is the kind of teacher—the kind of man—whose appearance in the hospital room of a middling student comes as no surprise. Gaunt and formal, Jarboe always wears a tie in class except during his free period, when he can be spotted stripped down to a plain white T-shirt, which happens to be the attire for his visit. In the days before the injury, Jarboe reminds him, they had closed discussion of *A Separate Peace* and moved on to the module in Existentialism. Freedom to act on your own choices, the ultimate responsibility of who you are lies with you. The question of authenticity, and the absolute freedom to create oneself—free of the excuse of genetic cause or the influences and expectations of others—presents challenges that he will wrestle with for decades to come. Sometimes Mr. Jarboe allows students to write papers on books of their own selection, so long as he has read them too, and this had led to three days of discussing the merits of *The Hitchhiker's Guide* as genre and as literature. "He felt that his whole life was some kind of dream and he sometimes wondered whose it was and whether they were enjoying it," and "We demand rigidly defined areas of doubt and uncertainty!" remained scrawled on the top left-hand side of the room-length chalkboard for nearly the entire first semester.

Existentialism might seem a little abstract and advanced for students in their early teens, Jarboe admitted after fielding many complaints, but he believed it was worth a look to get a handle on now as he could guarantee they'll be exposed to it again and again in the following years, particularly those going to college. Besides that, it was the most important and relevant philosophical idea of the age. Jarboe has brought a dittoed copy of Kafka's "The Metamorphosis" and an edition of *The Plague* in case he didn't have one at hand in the hospital, and tells him he's impressed to see a copy of the book on the bed stand; a bookmark juts out nearly halfway through the text, but the boy only happened to slip it in there to have one ready when he actually got around to starting to read.

So Jarboe tries to talk about a Camus that has yet to be accessed. Instead of making this become obvious, the boy gets him to talk some more about *A Separate Peace*, like why that title, and what do you think about that line Phineas uses after Gene asks why he's so sure the war in Europe isn't real, that it's a concoction created by wealthy white men to keep the little people in their places: "Because I've suffered," Phineas says. Is that intended as comedy, or is he being serious? Mr. Jarboe asks why he thinks the book begins with Gene visiting the school fifteen years after that fact, thus making the novel one long recollection and never returning to his adult life again once he starts on that summer of 1942. The boy admits he doesn't know. I'm talking about form, says Mr. Jarboe, who then goes on to explain how the older Gene can know things, take a perspective on events that the younger Gene, experiencing those events in real time, cannot. How this perspective deepens the resonance of what otherwise would be boys at play that ends up as tragedy, a book written for young readers only, which Mr. Jarboe believes *A Separate Peace* is not—it can be enjoyed by the young, true, that's why he assigns it to his classes, but the book is directed toward any adult reader as well, those who can appreciate the depth of the themes Knowles explored there. The sadness of tone, he believes, speaks to heart of any semi-intelligent, self-aware, adult reader.

If you took out the context of the war waiting for them, then it becomes a totally different novel, the boy says. He hadn't thought of this until now. Jarboe smiles, inclines his head; Boy Wonder is terribly pleased with himself. Even from a hospital bed, he can think.

One faction of the class—a small but vocal one—had argued that Phineas as a character was too good to be believed. Jarboe confesses he has had trouble with this facet himself, but believes it to be a minor issue, and he still assigns the novel because it's an excellent example for showing the way novels can work, with its obvious symbols (the Tree, the Fall of Man) and dichotomies (War / Peace; loyalty / betrayal; innocence / experience).

He hesitates to tell the teacher that, believable or not, he identifies with Phineas. And then he makes a move he would never have tried in the classroom, surrounded by others: he disagrees with Jarboe's assessment of Finny as a character.

He has thought about this. Of course Phineas is a fictional creation and so isn't real like Mr. Jarboe is. But the author didn't create Phineas out of nothing—he must have had experiences in the real world from which to draw on, right? Either a boy he knew or a projection of himself or maybe he used an aggregate of several boys, transforming them into Phineas on the page. Therefore there must have been an original, or several originals, in the real world. And surely he's not the only young reader to have fallen under Finny's spell, vowing to become more like him; since the book came out over two decades before, there must be thousands of versions of Phineas in the real world.

What he doesn't tell Mr. Jarboe is none of those versions can be precisely like him; he feels he is Finny's best and truest reader. *A Separate Peace*, fundamentally, is about him. A kind of distorted autobiography.

After a week a physical therapist begins to work on his legs, getting him out of bed and teaching him how to use a walker first, then crutches, and how to hold his leg so that he doesn't disrupt the healing by moving abruptly or catching his foot on a step. There is a strange piece of technology, too, like something out of a science fiction novel, this small box the size of a cigarette pack that connects electrodes to four different places on his hip and thigh. The machine sends ramping waves varied with short bursts of electricity through his flesh, depending on it settings. This stimulates blood flow, which aids healing, and also blocks the nerve signals transmitting pain to his brain. But more interesting is what he shows off to his brother, and then to Gary Thompson once he returns to school: if he places the electrodes a certain way and then increases the signal, all the muscles in his thigh twitch and jump like a fish out of water.

It's good to be back at school—a feeling he never would have been able to imagine before. It's good to hear of the stories that circulated after his injury, like the one that had it that he'd broken a rib and punctured his liver and was in the hospital fighting for his life. For the first few days after his return he enjoys a level of celebrity and camaraderie—even from teachers—that he can always punctuate with a demonstration of the machine attached to his belt, upperclassmen and football players stopping him in the hall to see the kid with the "bionic leg."

It's not all great, though; he'll learn over the years that no return ever is. The day comes when he asks Gary Thompson why he never came to visit. They're in a corner of the lunchroom. Gary admits he's not even supposed to be sitting with him there, or anywhere else in the school; his mother has forbidden him to have further contact with that boy who dragged him out of the house and into trouble that night weeks before. Gary says he's sorry, he wanted to come see him, especially once he heard about the rib and the liver; he wanted to call, but couldn't; even his little sister is mad at him because when the older brother returning from work caught up and tackled him, the impact broke several spokes and tore off the rear fender from her bike.

It feels like he's being dumped by a girl in whom he has placed his full adolescent heart. A burn at the edges of his eyes surprises him in its fervor, and he dials up the machine to watch his muscles pop in haywire rhythm for a painful distraction.

Gary says they can still sign up to become federal agents or spies. And his mom won't know who he's talking to at school. They just need to give it time. Once the school year is over and summer comes and goes, his parents will forget who it was that had seduced their son into such trouble—a bona fide neighborhood scandal—and they'll be friends again then. Friends who by that time are driving cars and all that.

•

Over the course of his recovery he comes to suspect that he's just another boy after all, with nothing exemplary or special about him. At first the necessity of hiding his friendship with Gary adds an illicit charge to any moment they spend together, lunchtime, class time, after school, but over the rest of the school year he can detect his friend pulling away, his honest effort to be the good son. Often his friend's eyes avoid his own, and the drawings they trade slow to a trickle, and he feels an awful sorrow. He had thought he had been doing Gary a favor, pushing him to at least a small act of revenge. Now it's like he can picture the entire scene as it must have happened after they were caught that night: the disheveled father barefoot in sweatpants and undershirt sucking furiously at a cigarette while he pushes Gary forward toward home, asking what the hell did he think he was doing out there and when everybody's supposed to be sleeping, you got a problem with a bully you man up and take him face to face or else you let me know and I'll take care of it, I'm not raising some punk weasel kid who can only stand up for himself on the sly, and where did you get those eggs? Don't tell me you stole your mom's eggs out of our fridge, you want to tell me what you think you and your sister's going to eat for breakfast tomorrow? How's your mom going to feel if she can't feed you tomorrow, huh, I bet you never even thought about that.

His free hand, father-strong and massive, would clutch the back of Gary's neck while urging him homeward, the sweat of Gary's sallow skin shining sickly as they pass beneath the street light, eyes cast down and watching the bend in the front wheel of his sister's bike where he put his foot through the spokes as he tried to outrun the big angry brother, how the bend rubbed the tire against the front fork with every other step he took. Finally telling his father he didn't steal any eggs from Mom and his father shooting the spent smoke into the yard and exhaling a lungful as he says Well God bless but that doesn't change a damn thing right here now, does it. Inevitably Gary's parents would learn his friend's father was in jail and even though they don't know the particulars, the words *jail* and *prison* attached to his name suffice to demand their son avoid that boy at all costs.

He tells his friend he's sorry for getting him in such trouble, everything is cool between them as far as he's concerned, he understands what anyone has to do to please their parents. It's what Phineas would say. He tells of having started to reread *A Separate Peace* again rather than the Camus book—which Gary insists he make the effort to get to, as it's really good—and how he thinks their own story is kind of like in parallel to Phineas and Gene, and doesn't Gary think so? He starts to detail the connections between the boys in the book and the boys in the real world, how Gary is a good student and competitive that way, and how he allows himself (or used to) to get talked into cutting classes or climbing into the rafters above the auditorium stage or whatever, and allows his friend to copy answers to Algebra tests when needed. I tell you, it's like you're Gene and I'm Phineas, and isn't that kind of crazy to see that in a book written long before either of us was born?

Gary shrugs, tells him again what he had said in class: he doesn't believe in Phineas. And then Gary surprises him by saying he might want to consider how his injury, unlike Finny's, could be seen as a positive, an opportunity. That for a while there he was beginning to be as insufferable as the bone-head jocks on the football team, guys they used to make fun of. That before the injury he was beginning to get too brash, full of himself—Gary references the biography deal as example—and going on about making varsity—the only freshman to do so! Gary quotes, mimicking his voice so well that he understands how often he pointed out this detail. As if making varsity soccer was the be-all end-all that everyone else wanted and wished for. Leaving his house in the middle of the night just because he could, and felt like doing it, not giving a care what sort of trouble it might make for his brother. . . . This is selfish behavior, and not like Phineas at all.

Gary tells him he needs to learn to think before he acts—his mother had told him to say this. It's a common refrain at home. Even his brother had once said the same, his way of apology before locking him into his room.

But I've suffered, he says, slipping one arm over the handles of his bunched crutches. It's frustrating to be unable to pull a direct quote from the novel, but the uptick in one corner of Gary's mouth proves he understood the reference.

Next you'll say the arms race with Russia is a story made up by old men to keep us boys ready to fight, Gary tells him, a peace offering.

He feels he should be granted insights into important

aspects of life, mild revelations earned by the seriousness of his injury and the tedious weeks of recovery. There are none. His provisions so far include only pain, bursts of sweaty anxiety, and the disheartening experience of watching his teammates compete in the sport he loves above all others while he leans against his crutches away from the bench and nearer the touchline, wincing at every on-field mistake. Increasing the agony is a belief deep in his heart that insists he would not have made the same mistakes himself, and yet there he is powerless to even try for the chance to prove it. Maybe Gary's mother would be happy to hear that all he does now is think, without acting.

Afterward, long after their discussion, when he's home and in his room again, he replays what Gary told him, tries to move past the hurt of it, to actually listen. Again he sets aside the Camus in order to plunge again into the summer of 1942, if only for a little while.

This book has stirred something new in him. He recognizes this unfamiliar set of mind: rather than reflecting on what happened and to whom, he feels the first pulls of curiosity to know *how*. How did John Knowles go about creating boys so real? How did he know what was going to happen between them, and make this teenage reader care? The novel pulls him into a past that has never interested him before, and yet in its details he discerns his own world, as if somehow Knowles had stepped into his fifteen-year-old life and set it off slightly askew, pulling him from the inner-city public school surrounded by projects and pavement to a private one basking in the New England countryside. How did Knowles seduce the reader into identifying with characters so closely that they seem different components of the reader's self? And then, step by step, lure him into a broken heart?

He used to read solely *for* story: a mystery to be solved, an adventure to canter through, a strange and foreign world to explore. For diversion and entertainment. The hero / detective always a stand-in for himself, if his self were rougher, more worldly, and clever enough to spout witty comebacks to any insult. Admiring the detective was, in a way, admiring himself.

This book, however, leads him somewhere different. There is no hero; Phineas is only a young boy, after all, and hardly worldly and knowing. The story is quiet, without thrills. Is it that which makes it feel so tragic? Because of its prosaic nature so close to his own day to day life, is that why? What's different is that he's captured less by the story and more by the people who happen to move through it; he's moved by this turn in their lives. *A Separate Peace* compels him to think—about himself and the person he believes himself to be, and about the world and what it may demand of him—and it's the first novel that prompts him to appreciate the artistry of its making. He doesn't have the language to talk about this in specific terms. But he believes he's beginning to see the conscious hand of the novel's maker. The form itself, its inner workings, strike him as nothing less than revelation: writing a novel must be like making a sculpture, but in words, or how one seizes on linked patterns in creating a song, how certain tones vibrate in agreement and lead his fingers to form a chord on the guitar.

Once he mastered the basic open guitar chords he set to writing his own songs. What did he need to master to earn the permission—that self-appointed permission which is confidence—to try his hand at a story? He knows how to write a sentence. He likes to look up words in the dictionary to discover their exact meaning. He has lived a few experiences that might be interesting to read on paper. What else does he need?

He's uncertain what would be the more tremendous accomplishment: to play the guitar as well as Jimi Hendrix or Mark Knopfler, or dominate the sport of soccer like the Brazilian Zico or the French Michel Platini, or . . . or write a novel as effective and lasting as *A Separate Peace*. He's uncertain if he has to choose, or if he even has the option of choosing.

His adductor muscles flex with pulses running through the electrodes while he sits still and staring at the blank wall. He intensifies the current and winces at the fresh pain it brings, believing the harder the machine works, the faster he will heal. The pain's sharpness reminds him of his body's betrayal, the degree to which it has let him down, and with the reminder comes a hurt identical to the hurt that accompanies the discovery of betrayal by your closest friend.

He opens the book again, starting over at page one, read now so many times that he can quote the opening lines: *I went back to Devon School not long ago. . . .* A door somewhere inside him, never noticed before, swings open. Maybe he could try writing about the friendship put on hold by Gary's parents; maybe by detailing the events of that night on the bikes with the eggs he can show Gary what he meant by the two of them being like Phineas and Gene. He sets the book aside and opens a battered spiral notebook, with pages that have to be smoothed into place with each turn due to the smashed wire spine so disfigured from being thrown in and out of his book bag, stepped on once or twice in the bus aisles as well.

When his mother raps on his door to call time on his studies and to get ready for bed, he is shocked to learn that well over two hours have passed. He looks back through the notebook and finds pages and pages filled with handwriting, both front and back sides and easily more pages than he has ever filled for any homework assignment. In his head he feels an utterly unfamiliar calm. It's almost as though he doesn't know where he's been, as though he had disappeared for a time. Where did all these words come from?

He's uncertain of what has been accomplished—if anything has been accomplished—but he likes the equanimity in his head. It feels good; *he* feels good. He takes a flashlight to bed and under the covers reads over what he has written. The words there transport him again to that night of so much trouble, and he's surprised to see how much he remembered in detail, the feel of his thumbnail scraped across the window screen, the simultaneous taste and smell of Gary's sleep-dried breath on his face as he spoke with their heads inches apart in the window.

He's too tired to read over everything; his eyes weary at deciphering his own wild scrawl for pages and pages, and he allows his head to fall back and sink toward sleep. He notes again the strange calm in his brain and wonders why he feels this way. And then his head recalls a line as if in answer, taken from this novel that seems to have been written expressly for him. It's what Phineas claims about summer:

When you really love something, then it loves you back.

THIRTY-TWO YEARS LIE BETWEEN THIS WRITING AND MY LAST reading of *A Separate Peace*. A curious situation developed over the course of that time: despite my conscious acknowledgment of the novel as primary, a deeply loved, eye-opening, formative book in my personal history, a strange resistance to opening it again grew in me, a conflicted opposition that gained equal weight in counter-balance to the weight of the book's personal importance. As my reading receded farther and farther into my past, this weird resistance-versus-significance scenario only increased. Many times as I scanned my shelves and my eye caught on the familiar spine, I would flip through the pages while wondering if the words there would hold up for me now—could the novel withstand my little arsenal of reading tactics and techniques? Would it even still speak to me, to whatever remnant of my teenage mind remained? No sooner did I reach for the book than this aversion would assert itself, as strong as an allergic reaction. Perhaps a part of me understood I was no longer open to what the book had to say. Or maybe the reverence the book maintained in my memory—a reverence deepened the longer I stayed away—actually worked *against* my interest in reading it again, since no book could likely meet the expectations this one had gained; revisiting it could lead only to disappointment. Usually, after years away, a return to some important place absorbed in youth surprises us with how much smaller it appears than what's in our memory. A school loses its intimidation; a bedroom appears impossibly cramped.

The stylistic restraint of Knowles's prose—perhaps the salient characteristic of the author's work—and the calm interior quality of narrator Gene's voice had settled me as a teenager, convinced me of the seriousness of the endeavor. This was an important book telling me important things that I needed to know intimately and immediately. Yet now the sentences I scan read as still-born, flat, uninspired. The machinations of the novel's structure, stocked with apparent foreshadowings and a host of familiar compare / contrast dualities (war vs peace, loyalty vs betrayal, guilt vs innocence, et cetera et cetera), the overt symbolism that had once given me a firm foothold from which to grasp the kind of formal architecture that made novels work (and which also suggested why some were more "important" than others), now felt contrived, restrictive. Rather than being moved by the humanity rendered in its pages, I detected an under-wrought brittleness and forceful didacticism—that smack of enforced emotional commitment that those of us who grew up in the seventies and eighties will recognize from the after-school specials on television.

Once I overcame these doubts and did speed through the text again, I was left nonplussed by all the baggage I'd foisted on this brief book. To a degree I could say the sly suspicion in the back of my head that for years had warned me away from returning to *A Separate Peace* had been proved correct; what I encountered though was no YA embarrassment but an effort much like every novel: a fallible human being had written this, and thereby managed a balance of successes and failures in the attempt.

Freed from all the pent-up expectations and assumptions that had amassed over decades, I was then able to try the novel again, this time ready to meet Knowles on his own terms. And this time I finished with a degree of cautious admiration for the author's accomplishment. Yes, the obvious nature of the novel's symbols and dualities still struck me as over-planned—almost as though the book had been designed as a primer for high school students learning to approach novel-length fiction for the purpose of discussion and term papers—but not so contrived as to destroy the experience. Knowles created a work worthy of admiration (especially so when you realize it was his first, or at least first published), full stop.

Still, disappointment followed my reading. Not from any weakness inherent to the novel itself, but for a recognition in its reader. I came away with my great respect for the novel still intact, but I no longer loved it.

Obviously *A Separate Peace* hasn't changed since high school; I have. Perhaps that's what spurred my resistance during all those years of glancing over the spine and then moving on.

•

Reading as a novelist changes every encounter with narrative at a variety of levels. Not all of these changes are for the better, and they can get in the way of the primary pleasure of reading for the enjoyment of a purposeful story peopled by vivid and interesting characters. I crack open a book and the novelist in me immediately begins to assess and evaluate: What is this writer doing? If I were to have picked up this book without any knowledge of the story or its author, would I still be intrigued enough to read beyond the initial pages (i.e., what in the language or presentation or events captures my interest, what power of authority does the narrative display)? Craft issues. Henry James wrote that in evaluating a work of fiction he employed three stages, asking (1) What is the author trying to accomplish? (2) Was the author successful in meeting that accomplishment? and (3) Was it worth doing in the first place? By habit I've taken this agenda to heart, and use it not only to evaluate the the work as a whole but also to salient aspects of it, to specific scenes, the opening, the ending, or whenever my mind begins to drift from the text.

Why does the story open in this way, with these verb tenses, this narrative stance, point of view, et cetera et cetera and often ad nauseam. If the novelist has won me over—and it takes a fairly incompetent or super-commercial writer (often the same thing) to fail to seduce me over the span of the first twenty or forty pages, as I'm usually a willing victim open to whatever a novelist is up for, always ready to be wowed and readily inclined to give the time necessary for the wowing—then quickly my reading experience vaults from basic what-and-why's to how, a kind of hopeful cribbing, in search of clues that might better my own work.

Reading in this fashion has been going on long enough that I no longer question its purpose or usefulness or even its rationality; it just is. And I wasn't sure I wanted to encounter John Knowles's novel in such fashion, even as I knew I was going to for the purposes of this book. Some books, in order to be properly appreciated, need to be encountered at a certain age and time in the life of the reader. It seems to me that, for a handful of American classics especially—Twain, Salinger, Knowles, Washington Irving, and Poe, to mention a few—adolescence, or at least a youthful mind, is the best moment to appreciate what they offer. Not to suggest adults can't respond to these works, but to youth they connect with a greater intensity; they meet readers with news that still echoes with the new. Reading these works as an adult, the charms on offer connect to remembered states of being—one reads them almost with nostalgia, even if opening the book for the first time. The connection isn't as direct. As teenagers we hunger for a better grip on what's happening to us and what still lies in wait. A less diplomatic way of putting this would be to say that, in general and maybe primarily from a teenager's perspective, the books that feel important to young American readers are the ones that are about us.

For example, somehow I managed to get through high school without reading Salinger's *The Catcher in the Rye*. In retrospect this seems impossible; to go through English and Humanities classes when I did, Knowles and Salinger and Kerouac embodied a bedrock triad that everyone had read by the time they started college. Over the years following high school I came to feel I was possibly the only person not to have read *Catcher;* even friends who were not regular readers had read at least that book. This led to such self-consciousness about my failure that, rather than picking up a copy to steam through in order to see for myself what everyone either intensely loved or loathed (no middling response seemed an option), a defiance grew within me so strongly that I made a point of *not* reading Salinger. However, his was an acknowledged classic and common cultural touchstone and was fairly inescapable—most of my fellow writer friends expressed dismay at my ignorance and unbelieving self-righteousness at my indifference to this fundamental American novel. Even Samuel Beckett, a hero of mine, praised *Catcher*, writing in a letter to a friend: "I liked it very much indeed, more than anything for a long time." Thus there came a time in my late twenties, well after a wary acceptance of writing fiction as the vocation that gave my life structure and purpose, to see what I'd missed. It helped that the book could be read in a single extended sitting.

Expectations were high. There should be much to glean from a novel that had engendered such widespread respect and influence. I went in prepared to be enthralled. The initial charge and charm of the opening pages inspired in me a tasteful regret, a regret welcomed in order to be overcome for having knowingly missed such an energetic work and for so long. How had I avoided this great book? Yet by the end I'd grown impatient. Impatient not only with the novel but with its author as well. Only conscious effort prevented me from hurrying through to the end, believing that, to be fair and objective, one has to meet a novel fully on its own terms. Still I was glad to finish with the experience: the novel failed me, apparently. No, correct that: I had failed the novel. Throughout the second half of the book Holden Caulfield's fears and hopes proved tedious, even as I recognized most everything he said as reflective of my teenage self. And it was exactly that reflection that made Caulfield tedious to me: these concerns no longer held my interest. *Catcher in the Rye* is pervasively adolescent. I felt the regret of a missed chance—my fifteen-year-old self would have loved Holden and all he had to say about phoniness and the crummy. But as an adult meeting him for the first time I could only visit his story and its anxieties and remember; I couldn't inhabit them, though, or him.

Perhaps the voice was new when the book first came out. It's difficult to speculate otherwise why Beckett, always on in search of the new, would have admired it. Perhaps the narrative stance—one long monologue—was what had attracted him; he found monologue a liberating form, employing the technique in nearly all of the prose works he considered his "better failures."

That regret of having missed the proper moment to encounter *Catcher* surely spurred my hesitation to revisit *A Separate Peace* after so many years. Who wants to second-guess what he once loved? It did not seem fair to ask the book to prove that it had deserved to be floating around in my head all this time; it had accomplished an enormous amount in my life already. Maybe my unconscious worried that to dislike the novel now would imply the pursuit of a literary life had been a mistake; I might recognize my impressionable adolescent self had been misled.

•

So why such autobiographical mining in a project ostensibly about another author's book? *A Separate Peace* has bobbed around in the back of my head for decades. Without ever returning to its pages, I've long credited the novel as a signal influence on my formation as a writer, perhaps even to my sensibility of what novels are designed to do. It's recognized as a classic *bildungsroman* (a genre of peculiar emphasis in American literature, it seems to me), and likewise it made a vague coming-of-age for me: for the first time, a work of literary art presupposed that my own experience, what little firsthand knowledge I had of the world, could be worthy material for art.

Before *A Separate Peace* made its way into my hands (as much as I articulated this line of thought to myself), my impression of the requirements to be an Author—the bona fides of the job—had been intensely Romantic. It's unclear when where or how these ideas took hold of me, but they seem widely held among those who do not write, and especially so by young readers who fantasize about the writing life. Early on and through high school the writers came with an aura of seasoned and sophisticated adventure about them, figures like Jack London, James Fenimore Cooper, Stephen Crane, Conrad, Remarque, Edgar Allan Poe, Twain, Hemingway. Kerouac. The Russians and Ancient Greeks. The murky profile in my head broke down somewhere along the following guidelines: the Author sought out experience in the wider world and made a point of bearing witness to Historic Events; he felt at home (it went without saying the Author was male) in the exotic. A global traveler, the Author journeyed by ship whenever possible, and into the hard places. He scoured the big cities and inspected foreign climes and mastered at least one other language—the more the better, likely the Romance languages or German. His personal history included a relentless series of unusual jobs, such as deckhand on the high seas (though river work would do), cartographic expeditions/exploration, war correspondent. A seedy fry cook or gruff bartender gig would suffice so long as the location proved brutal enough—Alaska or the heart of Africa, say. Or no job at all, chucking society to go hobo on the railways. Some firsthand experience of war of course, preferably on the battlefield as a soldier or medic, but a diplomatic position that doubled as cover for espionage would do as well. Comfortably familiar with small-town living and the demands of farm work. Of course the perfect scenario would have him raised in France, England, or Russia—really anywhere in Europe. Such were the prerequisites before permission to be an Author could be granted. Otherwise why would anyone believe he had a story to tell?

And then here comes a story of schoolboys who happen to be near my age. The narrator hails from West Virginia, a neighboring state I assumed mirrored my Kentucky world, just with more mountains. Here I'm given a story of friendship energized by mutual admiration and friendly rivalry just like that on the soccer field and swimming pool. Here we followed the commonplace intrigues between teenagers grappling with the same doubts and self-suspicions that greeted me every morning after the alarm clock, presented honestly and without irony—indeed presented as irony's opposite, the story delivered in an earnest seriousness tainted by the melancholy any thoughtful young man recognizes as the voice in his own head. And then somehow these everyday events in the lives of these ordinary boys culminate in a moment of real tragedy, the kind of life-or-death tragedy that ringed every thought I had at fifteen. (It was either bliss or despair for me then, and no middle ground.) And yet *ASP* did not read to me as a novel intended for children; one could detect a maturity in the telling. Moreover, the book came figuratively stamped as Classic Literature, pre-approved by the adult authorities who understood these things. A novel confirmed by time and teachers as fine enough to be taught in AP English class. So I could not presume the book spoke to me only because I was still a kid, despite how it revealed aspects of myself that had been scarcely glimpsed or suspected before. By the revealing, the book anointed these features as valid. *A Separate Peace* permitted me to see my adolescent life as serious and meaningful, holding significant weight, worthy of recognition in story. The stakes in life as I understood it mattered, and they were high.

Still, a paradox resides in my giving Knowles's novel such pride of place in my personal pantheon. I studied the book maybe a week or two longer than required for class and then never fully returned to its pages again. There is a substantial stack of favorite books I return to when seeking inspiration, examples of technique, ideas of structure or shape or stance. Or even simply to be reinvigorated by what literature can do. *A Separate Peace* is not one of them. And yet almost like a totem, my copy has traveled with me from home to college dorms to apartments, through years of living abroad, and into the home I have made with my wife—this mass-market paperback faded greatly with age, its pages brittle as marcescent leaves. Once or twice I've dipped into the opening again, or read through the boys' first afternoon with the great tree, and once revisited the mock trial the boys hold in the First Academy Building to inform the discussion of a similar scene with similar requirements in the work of a student. Otherwise the novel has been forever set aside, inhabiting that region of titles that maybe I'll get to again some day. Yet *A Separate*

Peace is included any time I swap lists of favorite titles with friends, and has often made for a reliable ice breaker, marking the first patch of common ground. "Oh of course, Finny!" we might say. "I was so upset when he died in the end." "Hell, I thought I was him." "Phineas and the tree." "The pink shirt!"

"That's the book that made me like books."

•

There are any number of books that I could lift from my shelves and declare formative to my sensibilities as a writer. Dostoevsky's "great five" novels have long provided crucial example, and for years I've made a point of rereading *Demons, Crime and Punishment,* or *The Brothers Karamazov* every winter. (Dostoevsky: not a summer read.) I can point to a distinct and direct influence in the case of *Demons,* in that its narrative stance suggested a model I employed to different affect and ends in the novel *Our Napoleon in Rags.* Anton Lavrent'evich G—v, the narrator of *Demons,* is generally regarded as a weakness in the novel's conception. He writes the book as a local historian, a kind of chronicler of gossip and rumor, whose self-appointed task is

> to describe the recent and very strange events that took place in our town, hitherto not remarkable for anything. . . . Let these details serve merely as an introduction to the chronicle presented here, while the story itself, which I am intending to relate, still lies ahead.

Yet once he gets past such "biographical details" regarding one of the novel's main characters, this narrator turns abstract and slips into the background; the narrative shifts to the more conventional omniscience employed by standard nineteenth-century European novels, with access to the thoughts and motivations of others and with scenes rife with dialogue depicted in straight-forward fashion despite the narrator not being present when these scenes occurred—thus displaying knowledge of a kind no mere observer could ever be privy to, only an inventing author (or God). Furthermore, the reader can be forgiven for forgetting the narrator even exists as such: long stretches of time and numerous pages pass without his commentary. Dostoevsky himself appears to forget Anton Lavrent'evich G—v is supposed to be writing out this "history," and tries to make up for his absence by breaking the narrative to make commentary from time to time, telling of how disturbing it was to hear of such and such scenes, or else darting off in search of one or another character in pursuit of developments, "the very strange events" occurring in his hitherto unremarkable town. Then he fades out again as these events overtake the novel's preoccupations.

It's the kind of grave mistake no workshop would allow a writer to get away with—imagine old Mr. Unpleasant Fyodor suffering the commentary from fellow students—and mars the novel's conception and execution. A sympathetic reader can excuse such clumsiness easily, for every other aspect of the novel is brilliant and, at times, thrilling. In Dostoevsky we are enticed to leave craft-oriented doubts at the door and just roll with whatever he's putting down on paper. And because he is Dostoevsky, the great storyteller with a genius vision of mankind, it's pretty easy to be persuaded. It might also help to know he perfected this narrative stance to outstanding effect in his next novel, *The Brothers Karamazov*. Still, sober analysis cannot avoid detecting the presence of Anton Lavrent'evich G—v as a major crack in the novel's foundation.

My own novel attempted to turn this tactic upside down. The majority of the text appears to follow the conventional third-person semi-omniscient point of view—the "free indirect style"—with each brief section anchored by a different primary character. This narrative perspective works as a kind of structural McGuffin, in that the story progresses toward an unveiling of a narrator, who is not who a reader might reasonably assume to be the novel's main character. What we believed was the novel's center turns out to be peripheral, and this small revelation encourages us to reflect on how this can be so while also casting the narrator's character in a different light—the narrative works as a kind of obscure local history as well as the formation of its narrator as a person of certain ideals. Hopefully, ideals the reader has taken into deep consideration and reflected upon by the point of the unveiling.

Much of the pleasure in writing that book lay in the difficulty of keeping to the challenge of Dostoevsky's narrative stance in *Demons*, learning from his example and identifying the risks while trying not to fall into the same traps: relating straight dialogue in scenes only where the narrator is present; never going so deeply into a character's interior life that couldn't be excused as speculation by an informed witness; relating events where the narrator wasn't present in ways that could be deduced as having had those scenes described to him by people who were there.

Honest novelists will admit that although their work might originate in personal experience—narrative ideas informed by the author's exposure to life—it is equally and as importantly true that books are born from other books. We return to the ones that matter to us to see how the work has been done. In his lovely poem "Axe Handles," Gary Snyder conjures an excellent metaphor for this process, addressing a quotation by Ezra Pound: "When making an axe handle / the pattern is not far off." The implication delves further into history as he writes, "I hear it again: / It's in Lu Ji's Wên Fu, fourth century / A.D. 'Essay on Literature'—in the / Preface: 'In making the handle / Of an axe / By cutting wood with an axe / The model is indeed near at hand.'" This is how stories are made, and how an artist of any stripe learns—returning to earlier examples in which similar invention was mastered.

I use the example of Dostoevsky and *Demons* to contrast my "use" or perspective on *A Separate Peace*. Though loved at one time, and remembered as loved, the novel hasn't provoked a narrative idea in me since the drafting of the first story I ever wrote. The one about the night when I coaxed Gary Thompson to get on his sister's bike so we could egg his bully's house. The story never earned a title or a second draft and remained in that battered spiral notebook which disappeared on me long ago.

Books I've returned to again and again not only for consolation but for artistic example, including Dostoevsky's great five: Paul Bowles's *The Spider's House* and *The Sheltering Sky;* Robert Stone's *Dog Soldiers, A Flag for Sunrise,* and *Damascus Gate;* everything by David Foster Wallace, but particularly the sections in *Infinite Jest* that involve the recovering

Demerol-addict Don Gately; Roberto Bolaño's *2666,* specifically the sections titled "The Part About Fate" and "The Part About Archimboldi"; Flannery O'Connor's entire oeuvre and the stories of David Means, Mark Richard, and Jayne Ann Phillips; Beckett's novels, and especially the shorter fiction collected by Penguin under the title *The Expelled and Other Novellas* ("First Love," and the tenuously linked trilogy "The Expelled," "The Calmative," and "The End"); the extraordinary essays of William Gass; *The Recognitions* and *JR* by William Gaddis, and, maybe most importantly, the perverse poetic world of Denis Johnson, who I think of as the Jimi Hendrix of American Lit. This list is not definitive. The titles included fluctuate in perpetuity, the list transforms and reverses hierarchy by whim and mood. I could be content to continue reacquainting myself with each book and author even as I question who has been left out (no Cormac McCarthy? DeLillo? Nabokov? Pynchon? Coetzee?), as a means toward pinpointing how and to what degree each has helped shape my small voice and vague scrimshawed "vision," but what's of interest to me here is that *A Separate Peace* isn't included. And yet this novel has for a lifetime maintained a place of high honor in my writer's conscience, the book that opened the door.

IN PREPARING THIS PROJECT I PERFORMED THE OBVIOUS first step with an eye toward supplying context: a Google search on the novel alone, and then another search on the author. I was curious to learn what-all is available out there on both subjects, and expected to find a great deal of thoughtful critical effort expended on a classic that has sold millions of copies since it appeared some fifty-six years ago. My connection to the book was personal, consisting of a single early phase in which I read the book repeatedly and then never returned to it again, and this made me feel ignorant of whatever reputation it (and its author) had earned in the meantime. What else had John Knowles written? *A Separate Peace* was his only book readily located in my memory, though I knew he had written others. Now that I had stopped to reflect on this novel and what it had meant to me, it felt odd to realize what little awareness I possessed regarding his other works, and what level of status, if any, his oeuvre had garnered in the literary world. "John Knowles" is not a name often dropped (or referenced) in the usual book chat found in the journals and magazines and author interviews that have made up a significant part of my reading life. This absence seems highly irregular and conspicuous, when one can readily assume that any American writer older than sixteen and younger than, say, seventy, has likely read his slim debut.

The assumption posited that the author and his books must be heralded somewhere, his prose an acknowledged influence honored by a cult audience; there would be dissections of his more ambitious novels, novelistic accomplishments measured and weighted alongside interviews from various stages of his life. I only happened to be unaware of these because my interests had drawn me to different literary climes. *A Separate Peace* was his first novel, after all; that my memory couldn't readily access the titles of his other books meant nothing, as even the most voracious reader suffers blind spots. New books could cease appearing tomorrow and still there wouldn't be enough time in a life to read all worth reading. In this spirit I searched with the expectation of discovering numerous essays and critiques, maybe even a career-spanning assessment such as can be found in the *New York Review of Books*. Any questions I might have after digesting these could likely be answered in whatever biographies were available.

These assumptions proved empty and the search results a surprise. Under his name only (taking care to exclude the other John Knowles revered for his fingerstyle work on acoustic guitar) one finds a promising 853,000 entries—but none of these consist of the kind of literary journalism or criticism I'd expected. Even the unavoidable *Wikipedia* page is distressingly short and generalized, and centers around *A Separate Peace* (which in turn has its own, more detailed entry), yet otherwise lists his published books (none of which receives its own entry) without any information aside from their publication dates. Much of what's there is little more than trivia, identifying the original person Knowles had used as the basis for the character Phineas and pointing to novelist Gore Vidal as a fellow student who had served as the basis for the character Brinker Hadley. Back to the online search you find a smattering of pull-quotes posted by fans on *GoodReads* and other quote-happy sites. But the sort of detailed consideration I sought does not exist aside from the study-guide primers produced for high school students in need of help with term papers once the novel has been assigned to them—*Spark Notes, CliffsNotes, Gradesaver,* and so on.

The book has long appealed to high school teachers not only because of the accessible ages of its main characters but also because *A Separate Peace* is a simple book to take apart and study. Beginning novelists especially can derive a solid example here of how to create a complex world from simple elements. The ubiquity of study guides identifying and explicating those elements steered me away from spending much time here discussing the usual literary aspects of the novel-as-artwork and focusing instead on the novel's personal effect where it intersected with my life. But it astounds me that the author of a novel so widely read and revered could also be so blankly ignored beyond that enforced encounter in high school. Think about it: what other literary fiction can match the number of copies that exist in the world or could be argued to have reached similar easy recognition in the wider culture? *Catcher in the Rye,* certainly, and *To Kill a Mockingbird,* and maybe *Catch-22* and *Lord of the Flies;* these novels (and their authors) enjoy much greater respect and attention, with plenty of serious criticism readily available. I couldn't find any Master's or PhD candidates writing their theses on the works of John Knowles; moreover, Google does not even surround Knowles with literature: the "People Also Search For" function lists Salinger as the fifth-closest name to his, whereas the others are those tenuously connected by their involvement in one of the two films made from *A Separate Peace*.

Unlike Salinger, Golding, Heller, or Lee, there is no book-length biography of John Knowles, despite his living to seventy-five years old and with a career of twelve books, each bearing the colophon of large New York publishers such as Macmillan and Random House. There is no website devoted to him; no long, detailed interviews. The ubiquitous Harold Bloom produced a volume for his *Bloom's Study Guides* series, which gives an overview of contemporary critical reactions to the book in question (contemporary to the book's publication), save for a more recent essay addressing the controversy of possible homosexual themes in the novel. In his very brief introduction Bloom calls it "most distinctly *the* Phillips Exeter Academy novel of our time," a backhanded compliment at best, narrowing the book's appeal drastically. The brevity of his introductory essay, less than five hundred words, indicates perhaps he too finds little to add about the novel than what has been written already.

•

Literary fashion is capricious, and John Knowles occupies a peculiar seat in our literature. He created one indisputable classic that has been read by successive generations; one could argue that, since 1960, a small part of coming-of-age in the United States meant reading the coming-of-age novel *A Separate Peace*. It has millions of copies in the US alone, has been filmed twice, and has inspired countless high school and college student essays. Knowing this, one might assume Knowles holds a concomitant seat as influential figure in American letters—an author with a slew of younger acolytes pointing to his work as inspiration to their own careers and ambitions. However, if Knowles occupies a throne in another writer's firmament, that writer isn't copping to it. Not publicly. Perhaps the closest we have is David Gilbert's recent and fine novel *& Sons*, which details the lives of the sons of one A. N. Dyer, a famous novelist whose first work sounds a lot like *A Separate Peace*.

However, back in the real world during his productive years, a new title by John Knowles received the type of review attention expected whenever a recognized author published a new book at a major house. Yet the interest appears to have stopped at these early newspaper reviews; any more thoughtful commentary is reserved for *A Separate Peace* only. When Knowles died in 2001, forty-one years after his first novel appeared, he merited a respectful 500-word obituary with photo in the *New York Times* (an obit that was then, tellingly, twice corrected on its details, which speaks to the descent from fame the author had undergone, the newspaper of record deciding the headline needed to identify him as the author of *ASP*, suspecting perhaps that without this few would have known who this Knowles person was). Only through such reviews and a smattering of profile articles can one try to glean the arc of Knowles's life and mark the reverberations his first novel sounded throughout its span. It's difficult to resist speculating by available evidence how *A Separate Peace,* with its enormous and never repeated success, affected the rest of his creative life—in terms of what he wrote and how it was received. The signs indicate he must have found it an albatross. From the comfortable seat of retrospection it appears Knowles may have lost his way and likely led a frustrated creative life, severely limited by the weight of public expectations, with nowhere to go but down after he just started.

His fiction appears to have drawn heavily from autobiographical sources. Born in Fairmont, West Virginia, to a life of privilege that he tried to play down in the few interviews and profiles available (his father was vice-president of a coal company at the time when coal was central to the nation's economy), Knowles attended the prestigious New Hampshire prep school Exeter Academy during World War II. Exeter, then a school for boys only, provided the obvious basis for the Devon boarding school in the novel. He resisted the experience at first, self-consciously undermined by the feeling that as a southerner he didn't belong. In 1972 he wrote a short essay for *The Exonian,* Exeter's weekly newspaper, reminiscing over the three years he attended there:

> I wasn't sure I liked the guys much ... too Eastern for me, too Yankee, too tough. They largely left me alone, and I them. [One] summer I realized I had fallen in love with Exeter. Most students don't experience summer there: I did so for two consecutive summers. . . . The great trees, the thick clinging ivy, the expanses of playing fields, the wind-

ing black-water river, the pure air all began to sort
of intoxicate me. Classroom windows were open;
the aroma of flowers and shrubbery floated in.
We were in shirt sleeves; the masters were relaxed.
Studies now were easy for me. The summer of 1943
at Exeter was as happy a time as I ever had in my
life.

He graduated in 1945 before the war ended and signed up
as a cadet in the Air Force, but he must not have stayed in the
military long, as he graduated from Yale University in 1949.
He married Beth Anne when he was only nineteen. At Yale he
wrote for the student newspaper, where one early assignment
had him covering a lecture given by Thornton Wilder, the
recipient of one Pulitzer for the novel *The Bridge of San Luis
Rey* and another for his play *Our Town*. Wilder happened to
live near the Yale campus and Knowles sought him out for an
interview, and the two got along well enough that Wilder soon
became his mentor, evaluating Knowles' nascent fiction and
guiding his efforts. After a brief stint as a reporter in Hartford,
Connecticut, Knowles lived in and traveled throughout Europe
and into the Middle East, making do as a freelance writer of
articles and short stories while also composing his first novel,
Descent into Proselito. This manuscript was strong enough to
find a publisher, and Knowles had it under contract already by
the time he shared it with Wilder. But his mentor responded
in a letter arguing that he didn't believe the novelist in Knowles
believed in what he was writing about, and advised that if he
was going to write a novel he needed to do so concerning
matters he really cared for, exploring subjects and themes that

honestly mattered to him. Knowles took this criticism to heart and withdrew the manuscript from the publisher (an action it seems impossible to imagine any first-time novelist doing today), and now the manuscript resides among the papers he donated to Exeter near the end of his life. *Descent into Proselito* has never appeared publicly, though it is available for research in the school's library.

He returned to the US late in the 1950s to take a position as editor at the travel magazine *Holiday*—a great gig for a budding (or even established) author. *Holiday* enjoyed a circulation of over a million copies per month, paid its writers well, and put Knowles in touch with such luminary contributors as Graham Greene, Jack Kerouac, and Truman Capote, with whom he became a lifetime friend. Working to gather material for a planned feature article, Knowles revisited the campus of Phillips Exeter, and there he became overwhelmed by nostalgia; in later years he would write of how it felt as though he had been transported in time to those summer sessions during the war, a time when he enjoyed a freedom deeply beyond what his adolescent awareness could grasp, a freedom he had never considered or even sought before. In this state of transport Knowles recognized a subject he cared about and knew well, as Wilder had advised. He set to work.

Over an early hour each morning he drafted 500 to 600 words before heading to the offices at *Holiday*. In 1985 he wrote an essay for the magazine *Esquire* upon the twenty-fifth anniversary of his book's publication, in which he claimed the novel to be the easiest project he ever undertook, admitting "[*A Separate Peace*] wrote itself. No book can have been easier to get down on paper." Often this sense of ease can mean the writer has become lazy, producing without judgment sentences as they appear—a charge leveled at the author regarding later books—but perhaps in Gene's voice Knowles heard his own, a voice he invoked naturally, as one of the great strengths in *ASP* is the grace and precision of its quiet sentences, maintaining a balanced restraint that never stumbles into a forced mannerism.

The novel's journey to publication follows the same distressingly familiar case of so many American classics. Why is it that no publisher wants to take the chance on a book that later proves itself great, and which seems so obviously accessible to its readers? What were the editors missing? Is there any American classic that was accepted for publication gladly? It's unclear if *A Separate Peace* was first submitted to fulfill the contract intended for *Proselito* and then refused, or if he had to pay back the advance received from that initial offering—either way, that press was included among the many who passed on the opportunity to publish the manuscript. Knowles did land a well-known literary agent, a feat that usually bodes well for a novel in search of a home, but in this case only added a fellow companion to suffer alongside the author as the rejections from every publishing house of note in the US arrived. An irony: *A Separate Peace*—this quintessentially American novel—first appeared in England. The British received it well there, too, giving laudatory reviews in their major papers and magazines. Only after seeing the novel's safe appearance in another country did a US publisher take notice, and what sweet satisfaction that must have been for Knowles, who was in his early thirties by this time and likely wondering if fiction still presented a legitimate career option. The American edition collected the kind of reviews that every writer dreams of and sold seven thousand copies, a respectful number for a first novel by an unknown author. More importantly, it was a number high enough for another publisher to buy the rights to a paperback edition.

The enormous success for which the book is recognized today—it's difficult to identify exact figures due to the various editions, but in his *Esquire* essay Knowles claimed the novel had sold over nine million copies, and that was thirty-five years ago—came gradually, over a span of years, after the novel made the syllabus of high schools everywhere. College courses, too, subsumed the accessible book. Students loved *ASP* for its readability and vivid characters, while teachers grew attached to its brevity, clear structure, and easy-to-spot symbolism. Perhaps its fame was helped by the cultural moment and the fact of the Vietnam war, wherein young readers caught parallels in this story of young boys alternately confronting, anticipating, and fleeing the war that awaited them. Many of those students would become teachers themselves, ready to introduce the novel to later generations.

But that sort of durable renown would come later. In the more immediate aftermath of the novel's appearance Knowles was hailed as the successor to Salinger, and the book received two of the most prestigious accolades available to it: the PEN/Faulkner award, given in honor of the best fiction written by a living American author, and the Rosenthal Award from the National Institute of Arts and Letters, which recognizes novels of "considerable literary achievement."

No writer could ask for a better introduction to a career. Both of the prizes mentioned have a pretty good track record for recognizing early works of authors who went on to become major figures in our literature. For example, since the award began in 1957, recipients of the Rosenthal include Thomas Pynchon, Marilynne Robinson, Richard Powers, Alice Walker, and Thomas McGuane—all novelists one suspects will have titles still in print for years after their deaths, and likely a biography or two. Fifteen years after Knowles passed away, however, *A Separate Peace* is his only book still in print, and this holds at a time when books don't really have to fall out of print anymore due to print-on-demand technology and digital editions. It's difficult not to conclude then that his other books aren't available because no one is interested in them.

So what happened?

•

> *The natural state of things is coldness, and houses are fragile havens, holdouts in a death landscape. . . .*
>
> —A Separate Peace

His reputation established, Knowles appears to have grasped the brass ring of achievement with such fervor that eventually it disintegrated in his hands. He was a disciplined worker, diligent and productive, publishing on a regular basis for another twenty-five years—yet over time he seems to have foundered, perhaps struggling to adhere to Wilder's advice and uncertain how to identify where his true interests lay, that center that allows a novelist to compose with confident authority over his material; he seems to have never developed that important sense that recognizes value (or none) in what one is writing. Each new novel garnered attention by the usual outlets such as the *New York Times* and its *Book Review,* often with a high-profile reviewer assigned, such as Paul Theroux or Michiko Kakutani. Searching out these articles in order to scan the vector of Knowles's career leads to some disappointing, often brutal, reading. Twenty-five years compressed into a few hours of study emphasizes a decrescendo of enthusiasm for what Knowles had on offer. At the outset the acclaim is bracing: Edmund Fuller in the *New York Times* opened his review of *A Separate Peace* with deep admiration, arguing that "Here is a first novel by a man already skilled in his craft and discerning in his perceptions. . . . [S]ensitive without being delicate, subtle without being obscure." He describes *ASP* as "a well-conceived, well-written novel, with levels of meaning not possible to explore briefly," and alludes to "major truths in [this] excellent book."

Two years later it was Fuller again to assess *Morning in Antibes.* He approached Knowles's follow-up with anticipation, and applauded the author's ambition in writing a completely different book "as worthwhile as the former." *Antibes* is a quiet mish-mash of influences, in my reading—imagine the F. Scott Fitzgerald of *Tender Is the Night* marinated in the styled preoccupations of Albert Camus, or perhaps Paul Bowles's explorations into the North African mind like that which can be found in *The Spider's House.* Decadent Americans pretend to aristocracy as they bask on the Riviera, where they've come to recuperate from failed marriages and yet seek to love again with adventurous abandon. Steep them in the contemporary political and social chaos of Algeria's near-civil war as it fought for independence from France, a conflict embodied by an Algerian immigrant "servant-companion" who serves as guide to the narrator's political education. Nothing about young boys in prep school in this one. The narrator and his ex-wife trade barbed remarks with the alacrity of characters in a Noël Coward play. The only feature in common with the earlier novel is that stance of a first-person narrator, though in *Antibes* his paralyzing self-consciousness makes him come off as static, a tepid observer who is never clearly defined even as he involves himself in the novel's action. Fuller found *Antibes* compelling if uneven—the story's thread of wealthy Americans and their love / lust lives appears grossly superficial when set against the political fire of the Algerian conflict and its effect on France (which may have been the author's aim); still, Fuller closes his assessment respectfully, impressed by the novel's implication that "the fight for love and reality is worth making, even in so artificial a context as the Riviera, that strange quiet eye at the center of a hurricane."

The fight for reality? I question the merit of such an assertion; reality imposes its victory upon all of us eventually. The copy of *Morning in Antibes* I managed to get my hands on shows the book did well enough to enter a third printing.

By 1962, now buoyed financially by the still-waxing success of *Peace,* Knowles took a break from fiction to travel, capturing his impressions in essays collected under the title *Double Vision: American Thoughts Abroad.* Here he presents himself as a romantically-inclined voyager in the mold of Gustave Flaubert, the flâneur searching for his own personal paradise and failing, perpetually disappointed in the realities on the ground wherever he goes. Some of his best writing can be found here. Knowles seems most comfortable writing as an observer, a contemplative and somewhat passive stance at one remove from the action, which allows him the space in which he reveals a sharp eye for physical detail and a conjuror's gift for evocative atmospheres. He is honest enough to admit that everywhere he goes, no matter how foreign and exotic and enchanting the new land may be, the traveler meets himself. And what sort of self must he be? An American, he writes. This judgment leads to rumination on the American character in general, particularized in the temperament he describes as "unintegrated, unresolved, a careful Protestant with a savage stirring in his insides." His insight to Western culture—not an especially illuminating or rare conclusion, having been explored and avowed by numerous novelists—is that beneath the calm, organized daily demeanor of modern civilization there lies "something berserk stirring in its depths." Knowles would make this theme the dominant feature of the novels that followed, sometimes forcing it into being on material that may not have naturally accepted such weight.

It's often said that most writers, especially American writers, have but a single vision of life to express; a handful of themes to stir the work; inborn obsessions that repeat and echo from book to book in varying manifestations—differentiated and discovered anew through changes in setting, time, and storyline, yet essentially remaining the same. The lucky writer unearths his furrow and mines it as deeply as he can: Hemingway and masculinity, say, or Faulkner and the weight of the past. Knowles's travel writing strikes the fundamental, anchoring note, the cantus firmus from which he builds new chords and melodies in all subsequent work. Here he hits upon the explicit fact of savagery hidden beneath rational exteriors as a primary concern (I was tempted to write *passion* instead of *concern*, but Knowles's restrained, often recalcitrant prose undermines the moods of passion; he is a supremely sober writer). An interested reader can scan his oeuvre and note a fellowship in situations, character types, and thematic pressures only a bird's breath away from those established in embryo in his first novel. He favored constrained settings—boarding schools, universities, military camps, small towns, hotel resorts; he uses few characters, preferring compressed, slim novels as opposed to the more expansive, and animates his characters by their individual degree of contrast between mild surface and wilder instincts. Perhaps his greatest strength lies in his ability to fuse the outside as mirror to the inside, by which I mean how he employs atmosphere and setting not only as decor and orientation but to underscore the interior lives of his characters. Much of his best writing, sentence by sentence, is located in descriptive passages of landscape and rooms—but also in his conveyance of complex worlds created from few elements. Recall the world cast in the pages of *A Separate Peace* and you can see how rich a milieu he managed to inscribe in your mind via the special hardness of marble steps, the height of a certain tree, two rivers, and a boy's pink shirt. Knowles worked with microcosms, intending a small part to stand in for the whole; a boarding school meant to stand in for a culture.

These same strengths also risk exposing weaknesses, however, if the structures employed feel mechanical and the fates of characters overly prescribed. An interior life at odds with the exterior day-to-day actions of a character is an excellent method for generating a character's plight, but then the challenge becomes—the fundamental challenge at the heart of creating fiction—to *dramatize* that character's transformation in real time. Contemporary readers, whether consciously or no, expect to easily accept the illusion that such transformations occur via free will, the unstated implication being that a character's destiny could have been entirely different were it not for the choices made in the face of circumstance. Without this, any narrative feels false. Characters aren't geometric vectors drawn for making a point (in good fiction, that is; prescribed vectors masquerading as characters run rampant throughout the world in bad books). In the kind of literary fiction Knowles worked within, protagonists (lesser characters as well) must undergo at least some degree of change, even if that change turns out to be only a hardened resistance to change; characters must travel some arc. Without this the narrative dream is broken and the work's overt contrivance betrays its aims and power. Everyone with more than a walk-on cameo has to have some skin in the game or else they don't belong.

Knowles' narrators are deliberators, witnesses. And usually men—the kind of men who mull things over a good while as they stand off to one side; often they are confidants of more enlivened personages, their narrative function along the same lines as Nick Carraway in *The Great Gatsby*. Over the duration of a John Knowles novel we follow these men as they contemplate their situation and consider its ramifications, men who ruminate over events rather than forcing them. A frequent criticism of his later novels accuses Knowles of writing *around* conflicts rather than setting loose their intrinsic passions; his passive narrators fret and reflect and struggle with the impetus of acting. The feeling is of a writer overly dedicated to discipline, constraint, and control. Perhaps his working method involved meticulous planning, all schisms and discords mapped out beforehand, and his process of actual writing involved the fleshing-out of strategies in place already. The risk in this method is to produce work that comes across as too pat, too evenly toned, obviously engineered and lacking fire. The reader rarely has the sense that the story ever surprised its writer.

As the works after *Double Vision* begin to appear, a simmering, hopeful impatience can be detected in critical reception. Once the impact of *A Separate Peace* recedes, the respectful tone of reviewers becomes mitigated by a sense of unmet expectations, moving from middling opinions ("such-and-such book has both positives and negatives," say) to outright derogatory dismissals by the time we reach his last few books. How could Knowles step away from the gravitational pull of his first novel? Perhaps, despite the financial freedom it gave him, he felt intimidated and constrained by *A Separate Peace* and its success, and grew to suspect the immense audience established by that book now brought demands of what he should give them—of what they could accept from him. Understandably he would wish to consolidate that large audience somehow, and so to stray too far from the fundamental elements comprising *ASP* posed risks he never felt comfortable making.

Of course it's equally possible that he didn't feel such pressures at all; he is described by more than one reporter as seemingly supremely self-confident. The steady income provided by *ASP* (he would call the book his "annuity") freed Knowles from the necessity of keeping a regular job to pay the bills and, though married, he did not have children, and so it appears he enjoyed all the time he needed to write whatever he wanted. Maybe he lacked the drive or vision to push himself into unfamiliar territory. He did feel it important to remain engaged with a literary community, especially among younger writers, stating that he found it "healthy" to "stay in touch with the younger generation—what they feel and think." From time to time, perhaps because he felt isolated and disengaged from such communities, or merely wanted an excuse to get away from his desk, he spent brief stints as a writer-in-residence at the University of North Carolina at Chapel Hill and at Princeton University. There's no information to be found on his qualities as a teacher, though he did admit his belief that writing fiction cannot be taught: "Everybody knows you can't teach anyone to write," Knowles told the *Florida Sun Sentinel* after he moved to Fort Lauderdale in the 1980s; he had accepted another writer-in-residence post at Florida Atlantic University, leading a six-week workshop course. "You can't instill talent. Talent is a gift, and it is bestowed capriciously. But there are technical insights that can be taught and can save students a great deal of time." Although he claimed that he had worked with some talented student writers in his workshops, none appear to have gone on to publish any work of note.

His third novel, *Indian Summer,* can be read as rather conservative in its artistic endeavor, keeping close to what had brought him success before. *Summer* hews closely in execution to *A Separate Peace*—taking elements from the earlier novel and setting them within a new context. He ages the Phineas character type and sets him loose in adulthood: Harold "Cleet" Kinsolving is a demobilized air force sergeant who feels boxed in with no war to let him run wild, a born nonconformist who creates his own rules. The so-called wildness underneath his civil exterior is rather programmatically and naively excused for his being a quarter Native American. The conventions of society, primarily the wealthy elite, chafe Kinsolving: he's forced to kowtow to a rich family in order to raise money for a business venture and works to re-establish a childhood friendship with that family's son, to whom near the end he realizes he has become subservient. Betrayal between two close friends, as in *ASP*, drives the narrative. The design is again conceived in simple terms, built upon a mirror-relationship between two males who are ostensibly loyal friends, the difference here being that the story unfolds from various points of view rather than by a single narrator. Unfortunately this disperses rather than widens the novel's effect. The youthful innocence that encourages such sympathetic reading of Gene and Finny does not translate well into the world of adults, and the inner dramatic possibilities for his characters gets lost beneath an overriding message that wealth can be a corrupting influence. There is another unexpected death, this time a stillborn child meant to represent hopes and dreams for the future. Life lessons are learned.

The New York Times describes *Indian Summer* as "a rich book, written with exuberance and an eccentric grace," yet one undermined by its seeming "unintegrated and uncertain of its own subject." The narrative slackens to loose ends, the early promise of its material never fully realized. Perhaps Knowles believed he was pushing himself into new territory and yet he couldn't resist hedging his bets, as it were, which leads unfortunately to a static model of a story rather than a vibrant engaging one. The novel's lukewarm reception was sobering, prompting him into a reconsideration of the scope and abilities of his readership and their fickle nature. He didn't believe *Indian Summer* was weaker than either of his other novels, and concluded that not every book can be a masterpiece, nor does it have the right to be received with welcome.

•

Knowles still remained popular enough to be included on the guest list to Truman Capote's famous Black and White Ball, the party for Katherine Graham that followed the publication of *In Cold Blood* and inspired John Lennon to write "Baby You're a Rich Man," which rhetorically needles the ball's attendees with the lines "how does it feel to be one of the beautiful people?/Now that we know who you are." Knowles had been a friend of Capote's since his time as an editor at *Holiday;* in the years following he complained to a reporter that whenever the two were out together, people would inevitably ask for Capote's autograph and never ask for his own—though surely at that time *ASP* had been read more widely than any of Capote's works. He published one more book to close out the sixties, the story collection *Phineas: Six Stories.* It's a minor effort, an obvious gesture meant to prod readers to recall his early celebrated novel, and an excuse to publish the eponymous story in book form—the story that had first appeared in *Cosmopolitan* in the 1950s, and which had served as starting point for the novel in which Phineas reaches full life.

A better reception greeted the release of *The Paragon* in 1971. "A beautiful, funny, moving novel about a young man in trouble," wrote critic Webster Schott. *Kirkus Reviews,* however, read the book differently, describing the main character Lou Colfax as "*another* [italics mine] of John Knowles' minor young men of good will and resilient if unresolved direction." Other reviewers reflected similar impressions, building to a consensus that recognized the work as one that has its small triumphs, a handful of successful scenes, but one whose ultimate effect feels scattershot and fails to cohere. The novel did not sell especially well. Its low numbers struck the author as an injustice. Perhaps it's about now that he starts to see his first novel's success as a weird kind of burden, recognizing the gap between what his audience expects from him and what he feels inclined to do; later in his life he estimates *The Paragon* to be one of his strongest accomplishments, one he wished more readers "had given a chance."

Still, an author has no choice but to forge ahead. Knowles persisted in his productive habits. Here I cannot help but wonder what he must have felt as he went about his working day throughout the seventies, the time in which he would likely consider the prime of his career, age-wise. Did he honestly believe, or did he have to convince himself, that this new manuscript was as good as his first—maybe the best he had ever made? Or was there a creeping dread, a sneaking suspicion that no one wanted anything from John Knowles except *A Separate Peace* again and again? Did the financial security of that book truly free him of such concerns, or did it confine him? Did he work on deadlines to fulfill contracts and thus couldn't allow himself to judge his material too harshly, recognizing that every novel has its weaknesses but the manuscript was due? Every writer wants to believe the most recent work is the best, but uncertainty is the only constant.

A profile in the *Los Angeles Times* which appeared in 1986 around the publication of his final novel, *The Private Life of Axie Reed*, describes Knowles as "an urbane, sophisticated man whose self-confidence borders on awe-inspiring"; but reading his reviews throughout the seventies one cannot help but suspect that *A Separate Peace* must have felt part of a distant past. And yet everything he writes is set in relation to that novel, and in this decade the usual organs of literary discussion begin to take on an almost aggressive edge. *ASP* is forever the context in which the new work is cast. Critics demarcate a line between that effort and everything else, and as succeeding novels fail to impress, questions begin to arise over whether the first novel still deserves its valued place in contemporary American letters. Critics speak to the difference between "admiring" a book as opposed to "loving" it. Whatever good will they may have felt for Knowles at the start of his career has now faded, and by the time his novel *Spreading Fires* appears in 1974, he is just another novelist plying away. Paul Theroux's evaluation of the new book steams with condescension; in his review he describes the continued popularity of *ASP* a "strange success," due mainly to its modesty of ambition. "Hideously overpraised for the doubtful virtue of being full of restraint," according to Theroux, although he makes no effort to clarify why a restrained style is a virtue or vice of any kind. He terms *A Separate Peace* "a novel in miniature," its clarity of expression easily gained because it did not attempt anything complicated. And although he goes on to praise the writer for expressing greater range in subsequent books (mentioning *Morning in Antibes* in particular, an unsurprising choice if one is familiar with Theroux's own preoccupations as a novelist, largely oriented toward travel and obscure foreign climes), the inescapable takeaway is that the knives are out. Knowles's curtailed, disciplined style, and his sometimes too-perfectly aligned structures, have fallen from fashion. He has become a conservative practitioner of the art, a traditionalist at a time when wild experimentation, black humor, and outright goofiness are in vogue—this is the heyday of Thomas Pynchon, John Gardner, Stanley Elkin, and William Gass, authors whose maximalist visions surge toward polar opposite aims to those Knowles felt drawn to as an artist.

A Vein of Riches follows in 1978. A more evidently autobiographical novel, it's set in West Virginia, and portrays a family who owns a coal mine during the labor fights that took place after the first world war. Now-familiar complaints greet the novel's release: protagonist Lyle Catherwood is called "*another* young identity-crisised hero from the John Knowles stable"; the narrative a "bland chronicle" bereft of anything "to give point and substance to a drippy boy or a droopy novel."

Knowles then responds with a return to the Devon school and the sepia-tinged world of *A Separate Peace* for the brief companion novel *Peace Breaks Out*. It's difficult not to see this as an attempt to stoke old fires, with Knowles seeking to reassert himself as a relevant artist desperate to remind readers of who he is and what he can do. The task requires dramatic risk on the author's part as it repeats the same setting and mood, employs similar character types, and is even structured with some of the same plot points that had worked so effectively in his first published novel.

It is as though Knowles made a conscious effort to create a derivative secondhand novel from one he had written long before. As though to announce he can make only a footnote to previous accomplishment. In this parable-like tale (with little in terms of psychological character development) he unsuccessfully tries to utilize the subtle ironies that sustain and enhance narrative drive in *ASP*, even as again the story is structured upon the tension between two students of opposite characteristics posed against one another. This time the conflict is between a voluble purveyor of democratic liberty against another who gives sympathetic voice to the forces the country had gone to war against in order to overcome. Clearly the story is designed to impart a moral: the inescapable truth of mankind's instinctual violence. Set in 1946, *Peace Breaks Out* seeks to portray the "incipient monsters" within the human, dramatizing the wayward instincts of adolescent boys with no war hanging over them to guide their needs for violence (the unintended implication being, one can argue, that war is thus a necessary pressure valve to be used for the proper growth of adolescent boys). Wexford is the popular editor of the school newspaper, a boy who enjoys debate and frets over the future of America now that the good war is over—he argues that the causes of that war reside in the heart forever and are inextricable from human nature; one's very purpose is to remain vigilant toward such natural urges. His classmate Hochschwender counters with Fascist opinions, even going so far as to praise some of Hitler's ideas. This, in 1946, just after the end of the most bitter war ever (Hochschwender is not a popular boy on campus). Presiding over the two is narrator Paul Hallam, a former student who has returned from his

POW experience to teach American History, a man who fits the John Knowles archetype of quiet observer, one who relates the actions of others without engaging in the conflict himself and who frets over the possible consequences until he concludes, finally, that there's nothing to be done. The confrontations between Wexford and Hochschwender escalate to the point of murder, though the cause and circumstance and ultimate responsibility is left ambiguous; it is as if one boy appears to die from the Spirit of the Age.

Critics dismissed *Peace Breaks Out* for its unbelievable plot contrivances and easy moralizing, the narrative distant, remote, unengaging, and laden by cliché. One reviewer took the novel to be such an utter failure that he mused in print over what kind of editor would allow a respected author to sabotage his own reputation as strongly as Knowles had done to his own. That said, *Peace Breaks Out* has its admirers, with a small but distinct group of readers to be found online posting quotes from the text and discussing its charms and relevance, finding value in the "message" Knowles brings regarding capital-E Evil's implications, his primary insight being that even the world's greatest mass-murderers were once adolescents. The novel is also commonly listed as one of the two works for which John Knowles is recognized—yet it, too, like all the others save for his first, has been out of print for years.

Knowles himself claimed to be rather proud of the novel, placing it among the two he wished readers would have given more of a fair hearing. He must have felt deep discouragement by this point. Perhaps he tried to brace himself, to muster the courage to retain his self-confidence by drinking alcohol— there is an event in the author's life at this time that suggests he wasn't entirely content with how things were working out for him: in 1983 Knowles was involved in a drunk-driving accident in Southampton, on Long Island. The newspaper article quotes a hospital spokesman describing the author as "lucid, but he's a very sick man." Knowles wasn't badly injured—no one was—and even he admitted to police that he had had "no business driving" as he had consumed "six to eight" bourbons before getting on the road. Assuming those drinks were of a standard pour implies Knowles was at least a heavy drinker, as that amount of bourbon would render any moderate drinkers comatose for a few hours; it appears as though the author was not the healthiest or happiest of individuals.

He wrote two more novels, *A Stolen Past* (1983) and *The Private Life of Axie Reed* (1986), two books in which he explored the conventional theme of the tasks and burdens the past inflicts on the present. His last novel received one of the Michiko Kakutani full-arsenal, scorched earth, take-no-prisoners reviews in the *New York Times* on which she has made her terrifying reputation, and it's tempting to presume Knowles may have concluded that, after nearly thirty years of striving and failing to equal or surpass *A Separate Peace*, perhaps he had endured enough from reviewers and critics and should just fold up shop. Kakutani opens her review with faint praise of his earlier work—a common characteristic of her take-down evaluations—in order to emphasize the stirring height from where the author under consideration has fallen:

> Knowles demonstrated a durable, if slender, tal-
> ent for delineating the emotional geometry con-

necting members of certain rarefied worlds (prep school, Yale University, the Riviera) in deft, cooly-refined prose. *The Private Life of Axie Reed* also takes place against a backdrop of wealth and privilege . . . but it surprisingly evinces none of Mr. Knowles's usual gifts. The book is obvious, poorly written and perfunctory in both tone and execution. It reads like the sort of name-brand schlock novel one might buy at an airport, though it lacks the tarted-up sex scenes and epic length associated with that form.

Those last two sentences are painful to read even if you are not the author of the book. The review is substantial in length, and her judgments veer downward from there. Kakutani rips out sentences and phrases to prove the flat clichés in which Knowles was foundering, mocking the way he "dithers on" with empty observations along the lines of how the rich are different from the rest of us; she skewers the "tired, pat descriptions and cheap melodrama" that comprise the entire novel, which evidently she found has utterly no redeeming value. "Ridiculously superficial." "So near to caricature."

The final judgment: "[A] deadly bore."

The Los Angeles Times responded in kind. Also starting her review by invoking *A Separate Peace*, Mona Gable quotes a reviewer from that long-ago time as asking, "'Is he the successor to Salinger for whom we have been waiting for so long?'" Then, regarding the new book under consideration, she asserts that "Looking at John Knowles' latest and ninth novel, one could wonder who the reviewer is talking about."

Axie Reed moved quickly from entering the world to sailing into oblivion. Or maybe it only seems that way from reading the outright dismissal via the reviews and in light of knowing Knowles would not write another book the rest of his life. He was only fifty-nine at this time, when he moved to Fort Lauderdale, Florida, to get out of the East Coast publishing scene—no longer so committed to remain engaged with a literary "community" so ready to disparage his efforts. There he claimed to be working on an autobiography. Silence is all that remains from the sixteen years remaining to him. What he did with that last stretch of time is not readily available to research, and he seems not to have retreated so much as disappeared completely into private life. It's hard not to imagine the man depositing his royalties for a book he wrote thirty years before, then forty years, with a kind of rueful empty satisfaction as he watched each of his other books fall out of print. Whether this embittered him, or confused him, or allowed doubt to hack away at his confidence regarding the worth he had made of the time granted him, is information only those close to Knowles would have access to—but how would one not wonder, in his shoes, how could he not wonder how it was that he had managed to get one work perfectly right a single time, and so early? Would he take back any of his other books if he could? Would he have written any of them differently, given another chance? Or did he still maintain secured confidence that the other novels succeeded in their own uncommercial way, and their oblivion was due to the irresponsive audience out there who had failed them? Perhaps he felt that with the one classic keeping his name in the world it would be only a matter of time before some literary scholar would come along and retrieve those books from where they rested, the way Herman Melville's had been saved some forty years after his death. Or maybe the recurrent presence of *A Separate Peace* in the world sat well with him, as even in the disappointment over how the rest of his output had been received, still he recognized that striking the perfect note only one time is more than hordes of other novelists ever manage to do. Maybe these feelings and thoughts are there to be found in the supposed autobiography he claimed to be composing; it's possible that whatever he had drafted sits with the rest of his papers in the library at Philips Exeter. It doesn't appear that there is anyone left who would have known firsthand what he believed or hoped for; he seems to have led a solitary life, survived at his death only by his original immediate family members, two sisters and a brother.

•

It's legitimate to ask whether *A Separate Peace* will continue to be read by students getting their initial taste of adult literature. Having polled the handful of high school English teachers of my acquaintance, my understanding is that the book is not taught with the same frequency as it was in my own high school years. In fact not one of them have admitted to teaching it, and neither have any other teachers they know, though admittedly this is only mere anecdote, not scientific fact. The novel remains on the approved list of books teachers may use in class. Certainly the novel is still considered a classic, but is it a *living* classic, a text to be discovered and digested and discussed anew? Does it still speak to us?

I try to imagine the teenager of today searching for a foothold, a way to get engaged by a book assigned rather than subjectively selected. How faraway the world of *A Separate Peace* must seem to them now, how slow the days unfolding there in comparison to the speeding hours of their own experience; how earnest the boys' concerns and energies, how absolute their innocence, must feel. Though Gene and Phineas are both sixteen, they must come across as sheltered children in the view of an adolescent who has seen thousands of bodies strewn across monitor and movie screens, kids who often cannot even name the nations who are our enemies or even allies. The reality of war or even the threat of it, its costs and moral hazards, has been largely expunged from media and by the methods of modern warfare, requiring little more from society than inconsequential obligations, the majority of us who pledge allegiance to our troops and gratitude to our soldiers by sporting tiny ribbons on our lapels or cars. Also strange to the contemporary student's mind must be the amount of careless freedom the boys enjoy, rarely overseen by the the few adult presences that populate the novel, as opposed to the extreme organization of kids' lives today, the brevity of their opportunities to not be engrossed in some immediate medium. The world of *A Separate Peace* must feel as distant and foreign to a sixteen-year-old today as the classic Russians had seemed to my teenage self—not simply another world, but another planet entirely. In my own adolescence, Phineas and Gene were two boys that could have walked out of my own eighth-grade or freshman classroom; today they seem impossibly young, solemnly green and guileless in ways a twelve-year-old would sneer at now.

Still the text remains accessible in its language, and reveals deeply relevant truths presented clearly enough that even the average addled mind of today can take possession of them with a modicum of concentration. But only so long as the book finds its way into the reader's hands can it fit the requisite requirements to be the "right" book at the "right" time, as it was for me. Often for that moment to happen depends on some figure of authority, a trustworthy, well-respected teacher, to place the book squarely in front of its prospective reader with the admonition to give it a week.

Early on in the novel the adult Gene Forrester expresses a subtle lamentation; he writes that Devon feels more like a museum than a school to him, which was "exactly what it was for me, and what I did not want it to be." It's tempting to speak the same of the novel itself: I fall into those initial pages and swim among currents of two times carefully preserved, one time depicted in its pages and another being the time in which I first read them, both magnified by the increasing distance between us. Reading the novel again after so many years away felt as though I were touring the rooms of a natural history exhibit designed specifically for me, a museum designed to immerse its visitor not only in a world grown distant from the one in which we live today—the world that fed this one—but also as a space meant to return me to when Phineas and Gene were my peers, the three of us able to look at one another eye to eye; when it seemed both boys were speaking to and for me. But one always has to say goodbye to childhood friends. And the thing about museums, no matter how fascinating they may be, is that they are never difficult to exit and leave behind.